PYG

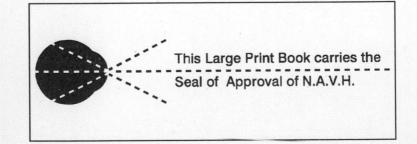

This Large Print Book carries the
Seal of Approval of N.A.V.H.

PYG

THE MEMOIRS OF TOBY, THE LEARNED PIG

EDITED BY RUSSELL POTTER

THORNDIKE PRESS
A part of Gale, Cengage Learning

GALE
CENGAGE Learning·

Detroit • New York • San Francisco • New Haven, Conn • Waterville, Maine • London

GALE
CENGAGE Learning®

LIBRARY OF CONGRESS CATALOGING-IN-PUBLICATION DATA

Potter, Russell A., 1960–
  Pyg : the memoirs of Toby, the learned pig / edited by Russell Potter.
  — Large print ed.
    p. cm. — (Thorndike Press large print reviewers' choice)
  ISBN-13: 978-1-4104-5208-5 (hardcover)
  ISBN-10: 1-4104-5208-5 (hardcover)
  1. Swine—Fiction. 2. Satire. 3. Large type books. I. Title. II. Title: Pig.
PS3616.O8525P95 2012b
813'.6—dc23   2012024628

Published in 2012 by arrangement with Penguin Books, a member of Penguin Group (USA) Inc.

Printed in the United States of America
1 2 3 4 5 6 7 16 15 14 13 12

For Karen Carr

il miglior fabbro

EDITOR'S NOTE

As the editor of this new edition of TOBY's autobiography, I should like to make a few brief remarks to those readers who may, by chance, take up this volume knowing nothing of the circumstances of its origin or first publication. You hold in your hands one of the most remarkable volumes ever to be published — indeed, the sole known *Memoir* of any creature of other than the Human race. Such a statement may at first seem to stretch the reader's credulity, but I hasten to assure you that this narrative requires no suspension of our ordinary notions of reality — only a realisation of how vast, indeed, that reality may be. The accomplishments of TOBY, in regard to his acquisition of Language, and his use of this ability in pursuit of writing a Narrative of his own, are too well documented to admit of any doubt. Many of the luminaries of the Eighteenth Century, the eminent Dr Johnson himself among them, attest to its veracity. As for the historical particulars, however, I shall leave these to the brief appendix that I have inserted after the main narrative, where those who are additionally curious may satisfy that most vital of all human impulses.

The text of the present volume is based on that of the first edition of 1809, which preserves what is by far the most authoritative text. Only three complete copies are known, one at the Bodleian (which was the copyright deposit), one in the library of the University of Edinburgh, and one in the National Library of Ireland in Dublin. Having compared and collated all of them, I can with assurance state that they are all from the identical impression, and contain no substantive variants besides the inevitable differences in the binding and trimming of the pages. The second printing of 1810, and all subsequent versions, are deficient not only in the main text, but in the great variety of spurious additions and emendations, more with each printing, which insert all manner of asides and comic interludes, so utterly different in tone and style from the original that I am quite certain they are the work of other hands (the more so as they continued to be added to subsequent editions well into the 1840s, by which time the original *Author* had long since expired). This is, therefore, the very first modern printing to contain the true and accurate account of TOBY's career, without any ornaments other than those that he gave it himself.

I have not altered the substance of the text in any way, and I have only modernised the punctuation as much as seemed absolutely necessary to retain the sense; the distinctive use of Capitalisation (quite common in its day) has been retained. It is to be hoped that this modest volume may earn for TOBY a new generation of readers, hitherto unacquainted with his adventures, who will find in them as curious and absorbing a mirror of *Nature* as did those who first perused these pages more than two centuries ago.

Russell Potter, Ph.D., MA, BA
October 2010

TO THE READER

ENDORSEMENT

I, *William Cullen,* MD, Fellow of the Royal Society, member of the Royal College of Physicians of Edinburgh, do hereby give my Attestation to the Truth of what follows. I have examined the Author of this Narrative on several occasions, entirely free from any Impediment or Collusion, and can Attest that, Unquestionably, the Narrator of this Tale is, Anatomically and in every Other Sense,
A PIG

1

When in Rome, do as the *Romans.* This adage, instilled within human children at a tender age, ensures the extension of a measure of courtesy and understanding to those whose ways are alien to one's own, and to that degree it is surely a *Wise* saying. But — and here I speak from painful experience — most who thus employ it scarce understand it. To demand that *Humans* regard other humans as being like themselves requires little Effort; such sympathy *within* the species is no more than any other Race of beings expects without a thought. For it is *only* among humans that other humans seem *less* than human; among Pigs (or any other Animal, I am sure), such conceits are utterly unknown. Indeed, I believe that throughout the Animal Kingdom, even and especially when one creature attacks and kills another, there is greater Courtesy extended, in each knowing the other to be a living, breathing thing much like itself, than the ordinary Human extends even to his *Friends.*

I myself was born in or about the year 1781 (as near as I have been able to ascertain), on a farm near Salford, a place not far from the great city of Manchester; so close to it, in fact, that I have since been told it has nearly become a *Suburb* of that Town. In my own day, its Character was entirely *Rural,* with a criss-cross of hedge-rows and pastures such as would be found in the most remote corner of the country. The whole Region was once known as the Hundred of Salford, which was practically a County in its own Right, and might well have become 'Salfordshire' had things worked out differently. My own birthplace was adjacent to the ancient manor of Boothes Hall, just to the North of what is now known as *Boothstown,* which still preserves something of its original character. My farm lay at the end of Lower New Row, though in my day it had no such name but was called, after its only destination, Lloyd Farm Lane. Mr Francis Lloyd was the owner of this farm and, after the fashion of the local Romans, *my* owner as well.

Mr Francis Lloyd was a Moderate man in every way: he was Moderately successful as a farmer, Moderate in his politics, Moderate in his treatment of his children, and Moderate in his drinking (which was limited to a Dram before dinner, excepting Sundays). He was not, alas, so Moderate in the treatment of his animals, but that would have been no surprise to his fellow Romans — animals *was* animals, and one would no more think of extending mercy or kindness to them than one would to a shrub, a stone, or a bit of Tallow. It was not that such creatures had no feelings — surely they did — but only that their feelings were simply not of account. The Squeal of a Piglet was doubtless the expression of *some* feeling or another, but most of all it was a Noise, a thing to be filtered out of one's hearing, much as the creak of a floorboard or the sound of wind in the trees. Mr Francis Lloyd raised Pigs to make money, same as he raised Barley or Cows — save that, in the case of the Cows, it was their Milk that was wanted rather than their Blood.

With some animals — horses, mostly — it has been the habit of Men to name, and keep some account of, a creature's Dam and Sire, if only to make a sort of Mathematics of success; a good Dam might be joined with a famous Sire to make another Champion to win the garland at the next St Leger Stakes. But when it comes to Pigs, men have long felt that there was little sense in naming them, as their only moment of Note was most commonly their being served for *Supper,* and found more flavourful or delicate than their predecessor — every one of them nameless save by such Ephemeral sobriquets as *Loin* or *Roast.* In such a realm of infinite and infinitely replaceable Parts, a row of Dinners one after another, the idea of naming any one such meal appeared as absurd as naming a toenail-clipping, or a Fart. On occasion, when some children from the neighbouring village came to call and wanted to see the pigs, the old Gaffer might call out cheerily to 'Grunter' or 'Stripe', but as soon as the moment had passed, the name was as forgotten as the dirt at the bottom of a bucket of pig swill. For who did not grunt, or had no stripe? We ourselves might as well have called men 'Two-legs' or 'Hair-head'.

In my own case, it is difficult to say exactly *when* I acquired my name. For, at the time 'Toby' was first bestowed upon me, it was as much a Noise to me as my grunts were to my masters; I had no idea of Language, or any association between such sounds and

18

my own Being. That Gift was later Bestowed upon me by a bright young lad of the name of Samuel Nicholson, Mr Lloyd's nephew, who was at the time living at his uncle's Farm. Sam was fond of pigs, and even without the aid of Language, this was instantly discernible to every Inhabitant of the Sty. Our Elders, who had lived long enough to see the previous generation sent to Slaughter, were of course more cautious than myself and the other younger Pigs, who swarmed about the edge of the Sty in competition for a proffered carrot. And, for reasons that to this day I cannot precisely Determine, Sam took a liking to me, and I to *Him.* Soon, he would Spy me out as soon as he neared the rail, and begin each Visit with some special treat — a slab of Cabbage, some Greens, or a slice of *Turnip* — intended only for me, after which he would toss a few kitchen scraps to the rest.

In part no doubt due to this favourable Treatment, I quickly grew to be the largest and ruddiest of my *Farrow* (a word then used to Signify the Pigs born alongside one). Sam was delighted with this, as indeed was Mr Francis Lloyd himself, though for *Opposite* reasons. For his part, Sam fancied that I would, after the fashion of a household Pet, soon come to his Call and form the sort of Intimacy that is common (for example) between Boys and Dogs; whereas Mr Francis Lloyd fancied that I might win the Ribbon at the Salford Horse and Live-stock Fair, and earn him a considerable Bonus per pound besides, when the time came after to sell me. As for Sam, he was, as I should express it now, of that very Age which cannot quite *Peep* over the Sill of adulthood but believes it to be little more than an Extension of childish existence — only on Tip-toes. Thus he had no conception whatsoever of these his Uncle's plans. And as for the Uncle — why, if there was a thing he thought *Less* of than his nephew's connections with one of his Pigs, I cannot imagine it.

2

There is scant Consolation, when regarding one's life with what *Humans,* who have a proclivity for accidental doublings of meaning, call 'Hind-sight', in saying that what happened was Necessary, and what was Necessary indeed *Happened.* And yet so it was with me: had it not been for the Fortuitous circumstance of Sam's youthful sentiment, there can be little doubt that, instead of this my *Book* before you on your Table, you would have a rasher of Bacon and a Rack of *Ribs* — and that these would be my only mortal remains. And even granted that, it was a far from Easy thing that I would be able to make my *Escape* with only a Boy of thirteen years as my Guide, for there were many matters still Hanging in the Balance without any of which, each occurring precisely as it did, I would with equal sureness have met the *Fate* intended by my owner. Among your kind, such things are quite commonly credited to Divine *Providence,* but as I recall, the good Lord dealt only once with Pigs — which was when he sent into them a Horde of *Demons,* causing them to leap off a Cliff to their Deaths — so I will, I hope, be forgiven if I do not give *Thanks* to that particular Source.

Now, as I say, my *Benefactor* — that is, young Samuel Nicholson — had no idea in his head of my being bid upon, or sent to be Slaughtered by the highest bidder. On the contrary, much as any other lad his Age, he regarded the Fair as chiefly an occasion for Amusement, for seeing Mr Punch strike Mistress Judy with his long stick, for taking in a Penny Gaff or a *Raree* show, for wandering the Gypsy stalls amidst great heaps of China plates, and — lastly — for a fine repast of ginger beer and Cake. Of course he had always known there were animals: of the three days of the Fair, one was set aside for Horses, one for Cows, and one for Pigs. Yet his wanderings never brought him to the Pens in which the animals were kept, nor to the auction-yards where they were bought and sold, and least of all to the far edge of the pitch where stood the great wagons, ready to bear their unlucky Passengers on their final Journey to some distant *Abattoir.*

In my own case, I was favoured by my owner with a stout and capacious Cart, with rails, that I might make my procession into Town in a manner likely to draw the admiration of other breeders and buyers. Sam took it into his head to decorate this cart, hanging streamers and bits of coloured Foil about its sides, along with a banner upon which he had written, in his own boyish hand, 'TOBY the Celebrated PIG'. Just what it was for which I was *Celebrated* he did not specify, but doubtless those who saw it made it out in this Sense: that I was celebrated for being *Young* and *Large,* and therefore sweet and succulent. Indeed, as the cart wound its way through the narrow, muddy streets of the market, Sam led the way with a Bell upon a stick, declaring, 'Make way! Make way! Make way for Toby, the Wonderful Pig!' He did not realise it, of course, but all this fuss was certain to have but one Effect — to raise the interest of the crowd, and to hasten my *Sale* to an Eager buyer. I myself did not quite discern the Danger since, as with all Pigs, our first trip to Market was generally our Last, but there were rumours enough among my Brothers and Sisters — and occasionally from the few older and wiser Pigs in the yard — that offered various Explanations, none of them *Pleasant,* for why none who Went had ever been known to Return.

From my Cart, I was unceremoniously turned out into a Pen, with the other contenders for the Prize. A Committee of three Judges, chosen from among those Farmers and Victuallers whose experience in the selling and buying of Pigs was longest, made their way round this pen, Examining each one of us — there were Ten in all — with a quite distressing sort of Professional eye. I was peered at, prodded, poked and pondered over; my Mouth was rudely forced open and my *Teeth* examined, and the same things were done to each of Us, to the great Interest of all present, which they signified with much muttering and grumbling. You would think that it was only by Degrees of dissatisfaction we were to be distinguished, to hear ourselves discussed in such Undertones, but apparently at this High level of appraisal, it was the Lack of Faults that was wanted, and this could not be measured without Counting each of them. I regard it as a great Blessing that I was not at that time acquainted with Human speech, or else I should have begun with a very *Poor* opinion of myself, which

24

might have prevented the Progress I was later able to make.

At length, when the judges were apparently satisfied that they had noted down every blemish upon our Characters and Physiognomy, they retired into a little booth to write down their judgment. When they returned, the most senior among them had a length of Blue ribbon in his hand, which he turned and presented — to my great consternation — to Mr Francis Lloyd! Sam, of course, was on his feet in an instant, cheering and proclaiming me the Champion of the Fair, but all I could wonder was Why, after it was *I* who had undergone such Irksome and provoking examinations, the *Ribbon* was to be given to my 'Owner' and not to me! It is a source of some comfort, despite its Manner of being awarded, that this Prize has since been returned to my Possession, and indeed lies before me now as I undertake to write this, my *Life*.

After a brief interval, the other Pigs were discharged to their Owners, and I was returned to my Cart, upon which Sam had affixed the prize Ribbon, for a further procession through the Fair, during which, like a new-Crowned *Monarch*, I received the Applause of my Subjects. All the while this was happening, however, Mr Francis Lloyd was busy talking with potential Buyers, and by the time I had completed my peregrinations, he had apparently settled upon a *Price*. I was then turned out into a small crate, that could scarcely accommodate me, then hoisted on a Balance with which I was duly Weighed, and found to amount to twenty stone, four pounds, a very good Sum, I have since been told, for a *Pig* under a year old. At the time, I had no notion of this, but was greatly Alarmed that I might be separated from my Benefactor, and looked about most anxiously for him. Sam, alas, had been detained by a group of his *Friends,* who proposed that my Championship be celebrated with a quaff of Ale they had procured for the occasion from a nearby Tavern, and as he had no idea of the *Danger* I was in, he happily accepted their Invitation. My attempt to look about was met with a harsh reproach from my new Owner, who promptly struck me with a Bamboo cane, causing me to squirm about so greatly that I Broke out from the weighing-box and, for a glorious moment, had my *Freedom*.

It was to be short-lived, as this man — whose name I later learnt was *Wilson* — was prepared for such Contingencies, and soon had me caught in a sort of Noose at the end of a Pole he kept handy for such Occasions. With this foul Instrument about my Neck, I was led up a narrow ramp into the enormous *Cart,* which he employed to bring home his new Purchases. I found myself in a dark enclosure, filled with bits of the most filthy *Straw,* amidst which were not a few of my Brother and Sister animals, in various states of shock and *Dismay.*

Now, it is a well-known Fact that *Humans,* being Sons of *Narcissus,* quite readily — and *kindly,* they imagine — extend the Mirror of their Sensibility to other *Creatures,* assigning them the same sort of feeling and Expression as Themselves. Thus, were they to describe such a Scene, they would make it out that the fellow-feeling among such a group would lead to instant Friendship, and mutual Pledges of assistance. But, of course, this was never *So;* we Pigs are Alien to such things, having no Idea, nor occasion to *Construct,* that which Men call a *Self.* In its place, we have only this poor conceit: that we live, we eat, we shudder and we *Die* to suit men's tables. Have we voice? None. Have we some sense of what is to Come? Indeed we do, but little it profits us. Most vitally, we have no more Acquaintance with such a Human thing as *Language* to either Possess or *Express* such feelings as the more feeling among Men attribute to us. So, in respect of these my Companions, as well as of Myself, I can say only that we possessed a common and a *Mute* terror that could not be Communicated if we would, save in squeals and grunts that would do no Justice, either to ourselves or to any *People* who chanced to hear it — and thus we remained *Silent.*

3

For a very long time, the cart remained Stationary, and gave at least the Comfort that no further Indignities were to be wrought upon us, but as the Sun declined outside, and the dark within Deepened, there came a series of most alarming *Sounds.* First, the Ramp, by which I had entered, was taken up, and stowed away; second, there was the clattering noise of a team of Horses being backed up and Hitched to the wagon. Similar yet fainter sounds in the Vicinity made it clear enough: the Fair was *Over,* and it was time now for the Purchasers to drive on with their *Purchases.* It was just at this Moment when, like an Angel's Clarion call from out of a dismal Cloud, I heard my Benefactor's voice raised aloud. I could not, of course, understand the *Sense* of his Utterances, but the

29

distress in his tone was clear; a moment later, I heard with it the voice of Mr Francis Lloyd, attempting to calm and then command his *Nephew* to silence. This resulted only in his greater cries, and harsher Remonstrances from the Uncle, amidst which the voice of Mr Wilson was soon added to the *Din.*

What the result of this Outcry might have been, I was never to know, for before it could conclude, Mr Wilson put the whip to his Horses and set off down the Lane at a Frightening rate. The voices faded into the distance, although it seemed to me that Sam's, for a moment at least, was endeavouring to keep Pace. Heedless of such pleas, my new Owner drove the wagon onwards as though it were a Fire-engine racing to extinguish some horrific *Blaze.* It was a good while later when, his horses snorting with exhaustion, the Lane growing every moment rougher and (so it seemed) more twisted, he was obliged to slow his Progress and, as we soon came to a steep incline, had for a time to Halt. The Wretchedness felt by those within would be impossible to Overstate; we had been tossed about among the foetid Straw, and hurled both against each *Other* and the walls of our Enclosure, so severely that we were much Bruised, and nearly knocked Senseless. And yet even in this Wounded state, I felt a great leaping in my heart as I detected, just a few inches from where I lay, the unmistakable sound of a Boy breathing.

I uttered no answering Cry, and gave no sign of Recognition, knowing without having to be told that it would be an *Awful* thing to disclose the presence of this youthful *Stowaway* to our infernal Conductor. And, indeed, it was not long before he once more cracked his *Whip* and sent us speeding over the hill and Down, with every living thing Careering about as though we were so much Laundry in a Mangle cranked by a *Madman.* It was nearly dawn, and I could just make out the singing of a Lark through the mire-spattered slats of my Confine, when we pulled into Mr Wilson's premises. I thought, too, that I could hear my Breathing boy, but with the rattle and ring of our Ride in my ears, I could not be absolutely certain. The sound of our Owner speaking with one of his *Hands,* and the sound of the horses being unhitched and led to his Stables, gave us at least a partial Augury of *Peace,* and I suppose that I must almost instantly have fallen Asleep. My next recollection was of being awakened by the sound of the Ramp as it was once more attached to our Enclosure, as the dim glimmer of the afternoon Sun painted stripes upon the floor. Up we went, and over, and were Herded by men with long Poles into a Pen, which was, if such were possible, more *Filthy* than our previous habitation. The belief that Pigs, simply because they appreciate the cooling properties of some lovely clean *Mud,* are therefore inured to any sort of Refuse, or even love to Gambol in *Faeces* or Garbage, has such wide circulation among Humans that we could scarce Dissuade them from it if we *Could* speak — and Mr Wilson's faith in this notion was stronger than Most. The stench that arose from the admixture of kitchen slops, manure and *Urine* suggested that this pen had not been cleaned out in many Months, if not Years.

Never the less, foul as it was, it was (at least) roofed with the *Sky* rather than the sharp boards of the wagon, and as long as there was even the slightest Breeze, it was considerably more pleasant and Commodious. I looked about at once for my *Benefactor,* and hoped that he had been able to Drop from the wagon and secrete himself in some quiet corner of the *Barn,* or find concealment within a convenient Bale of *Hay.* Just at that moment, I was most Rudely brought out of my Study, when a vast bucket of *Swill* — consisting of mouldy barley mixed with water and rotted vegetables — was Dumped between (or rather *Upon*) my comrades and me, and we were at some pains to devour some portion of it, before it was hopelessly mixed with the Mire. Let the *Human* who imagines this is Agreeable to *Pigs* take even the smallest quantity of this Stuff in his Cup — and he would surely be compelled to *Retch* even before the Rim reached his Lips.

Having finished what we could of this very *Disagreeable* meal, we all of us fell into a sort of Stupor, which for a time made me believe that our meal had been conjoined with some Opiate or other sleep-inducing *Drug.* I next woke in what seemed the stillest hour of the Night, with only the distant *Threnody* of autumnal insects, accompanied by the faint moan of the wind in the trees in my ears — or *was* it? Or *could* it be? It was. From just inside the large and ill-kept *Barn* that loomed over our Sty, I was certain I could detect the restless moaning of a Boy, who must surely be my Benefactor and my only *Friend.* But what could I do? Were I to break out of my confinement by *Force,* there would surely be a half-dozen men upon me in a moment, shouting and cursing, and Mr

Wilson with his bamboo *Cane* not far behind. I could make no sound, either, that would not have brought the same results, even if by some means I could gain his Attention.

Looking closely at the posts of the Fence that confined me, I observed that they had been fixed in the ground with a sort of very rough Cement, which contained a sort of greyish gravel. Quite a few bits of this had come loose, and were scattered about the base of each Post. With very little difficulty, by using my Snout, I was able to toss a few Skywards, whence they struck the corner of a small Window on the side of the Barn, making a very distinct sound. I repeated this gesture several Times, and was immensely pleased, a moment later, to see Sam's face peep above the Window-sill, and Spy me out. How I wished I could have communicated my *State,* along with a word or two of Caution, to him! Yet despite this Lack, I could see the lad had his Senses about him, and only smiled quietly through the cracked glass, then lowered his Head out of Sight. I was greatly Relieved, that at last we had some Means of alerting one another, and even though I could hardly then Imagine how we might effect our *Escape,* I instantly believed — with every contraction of my beating *Heart* — that somehow we would manage it.

The next morning, I was awakened by a fresh dousing of Swill, which the keeper — a shovel-faced lad of perhaps sixteen years — delighted in pouring over our heads so as to set us all in a Frenzy of feeding. I scarce partook of it, thinking only of how *Soon* I might be released from this my Bondage, and set upon my way in the World. And yet, only a Moment later, I beheld a thing that nearly *Stopt* the very Course of my Being! For there, down the lane in our direction, came a wagon whose sides were all whitewashed, driven by a tall man wearing a bloody Apron, a man whose function I immediately knew — if you will Pardon the Pun — in the most *Visceral* sense, was to Eviscerate us all. Apparently Mr Wilson, in every way a *Middle-man* in the great affair of buying and selling Live-stock, had little Stomach for the Slaughter, or perhaps simply felt that Butchering was best left to *Butchers.* And so at once, quite Heedless of the risk, I tossed up a great hail of Gravel upon the Barn window, without — I tremble to relate — the least Result. My Benefactor slept, I could only surmise, unaware of this Imminent Sentence upon my *Life,* and I must Risk all to arouse him.

There being no time to Consider other Alternatives, I began to leap and squeal at the very Top of my *Voice,* and to dash about my Pen as though I were in the final Fit of some awful distress; for at least, if I could not communicate my Situation, perhaps I could convince my new Owner that I was *Mad,* and therefore unfit for Human Consumption. The Butcher, however, paid no heed to this Demonstration, continuing along the gravel path to the great House, as though such things were all too Familiar in his trade, and soon disappearing behind the Gate. My outburst, however, finally had the Desired effect, of waking up young Sam from his straw-bed, and alerting him to the terrible *Danger* in which I stood.

He had only a Moment to think what to do, and his Wits did not desert him. He ran over to the pen and quickly lifted the rude Latch — consisting only of a bar of wood held fast by a rusted Nail. I at once leapt out from my confinement, and together we hurried down the lane. I should here note that, the larger part of Mr Wilson's farm being Pasture, a fence ran around its entire perimeter, with a *Gate* at the end of the Lane being the only place it could be Crossed. We made for this gate, my Benefactor somewhat unsteady on his feet (which was no *Wonder,* considering his journey here had been as Rough as ours, and I do not believe he had taken any Food), and myself labouring, unused as I was to the Exertions of any sort of *Journey* (having never had either occasion or ability to undertake one), and thus by the time we reached our Goal, we were both of us Exhausted.

At that very moment, we saw the Butcher and Mr Wilson emerge from the front of the House; we had only a very brief interval before they would round the corner and come upon the opened Pen, about which my former animal comrades were now milling quite Freely — and then they would surely *Spot* us.

Sam saw all this, same as me, and quickly lifted the latch of the Gate. I was already trotting down the next section of the lane, when I looked behind me and saw Sam had stayed behind; having closed the gate, he was tying a bit of twine about the latch, such that it could not easily be opened by our *Pursuers.* Already, I could hear Shouts, Mr Wilson's chief among them, and it seemed to me I could almost feel the crack of his horrible *Cane* upon my sides. Having finished his work, Sam broke into a run, and soon caught up with me. Just ahead of us, he spotted a small Gap in the thick Hedge that ran along one side of the road, and he quickly dashed through, beckoning me to follow. With some difficulty — the legs of a *Pig* being shorter and less limber than those of a Boy — I managed to enter as well, and we found ourselves in a small copse of trees, where Silence hung heavy as the dead leaves upon the Ground, absorbing any sound almost before it could be made. Sam quickly realized that such a natural *Bower,* dark and off the beaten Way, would be a far safer resting place than any open Field, and that we might — with luck — remain unseen while our Pursuers, in the heat of their anger, passed on down the *Road* unawares. He quickly scooped up some leaves and twigs, and with a little effort, managed to Cover me almost entirely; this accomplished, he pulled a similar *Blanket* over himself, and lay down pressed as tightly as he could to the ground, and to me. A moment later, we heard the rush and clatter of a passing Wagon, whose Noise was too well known to me to Mistake — and then the delightful sound of its foul Spokes and *Fellies* rattling and rotating away into *Nothing* in the distance. We slept, then.

4

Having been so earnestly desirous of finding my way through the World, I now discovered that it was a far Vaster and more Inhospitable place than I could ever have *Imagined.* For the Animal, once Domesticated, it must ever be thus: they have been made a place beside Man, and given a purpose in life quite Contrary to that assigned them by Nature; their Existence is not even properly their *Own.* I soon discovered that I was even *Less* at home in this New Life than I had been my *Last,* and I held out little hope that this Disjointure within the order of things could ever be Mended. My Benefactor, of course, was as kindly and Protective as he could possibly be, obtaining wild roots and herbs for me to Eat, and making each night a *Bed* for me upon the Heather. And yet, despite his good

Intentions, his small hands could hardly Gather anything approaching the quantity of Food to which I, a *Prize Pig,* had become accustomed; nor could I, having come from a *Line* that long ago had had its natural Talents bred out of it, manage any better for *Myself.*

Looking back, it is Remarkable to me that we endured as long as we did. I had, of course, no notion of Numbers or Dates at that time, but I should say it was a *Fortnight,* and perhaps even a few days more, before we finally stumbled upon that Place which was, for a time at least, to be a sort of Haven for us both. We had, so far as we were able, kept off the High roads, following a crooked path across pasture, heath and marshland. Occasionally, when Sam was able, he would Hide me in a convenient place, then Nip across a farmer's field and Glean a meagre meal for us both. It was late in the Year, and Winter would soon be coming on, which meant the pickings were Scarce, and our Situation daily grew more Perilous. I lost a good deal of the Weight I had so Famously acquired, and began, in Appearance at least, to resemble my Darker and Leaner ancestors. Sam, although never an especially Tidy lad, began to acquire such a Patina of dirt that you would have taken him for a *Gypsy,* or one of those boys who labour all day in a Coal-pit. We were indeed a Capital pair — the Wild Boy and the Wild Boar, we might well have been called — and our one comfort was that, if found, it would scarce be likely that anyone would Recognise us, or suspect our Origins.

It was while we were in this Dismal state that we came upon a large country farm which, even from a Distance, looked to be a step up from the rest. It was not just the well-kept buildings and pastures, though these were certainly Picturesque, but rather the curious appearance of the Creatures who dwelt therein that captured our attention. The Horses, which we spied First, were most Odd in their bearing: they walked with a certain deliberate trot, much as animals that have been trained for *Dressage,* and yet their manners seemed entirely Natural, as though they were executing a Dance of their own Design. Some years after this, I read of the singular race of *Houyhnhnms,* as described by Dean Swift, and had I known of them before, I would have sworn these were *They.* Coming closer, we beheld several Dogs that appeared to have the run of the Place and yet — again, in an uncannily Human sort of way — exhibited a curious sort of courtesy. When they passed, it seemed as though they did *Bow* to one another (that is, make a motion with their *Heads* not, as some delineate a dog's hallo, to say 'Bow Wow'), and they did Often rise up on their hind Quarters, and place their Paws upon a Rail or a Wall, standing in this posture for some Minutes on End. We were the more Amazed to see a great number of Cats, which appeared to dwell alongside the Dogs in perfect Harmony, as if there was no Reason in the World for any animosity between them.

Such a place stirred in us great Wonder, as well as (I must admit) a modicum of Fear. Had it not been for the extreme Lateness of the Season, the pinch of Winter being already at our *Heels* — and for the great Emptiness in our *Stomachs* — I doubt that we would have hazarded to draw nearer. And yet, by a sort of strange Fascination, nearer and nearer did we draw, until at last we attracted the attention of several of the Dogs. These creatures did not, to our Amazement, bark at us or attempt to drive us away, but instead ran quickly back toward the main House, emerging a few moments later in the company of the most singular Man I had then, or have ever since, Encountered.

This man — whose name, we would soon

learn, was Mr Silas Bisset — seemed as much or even More at home among his Animal comrades as he would in any Human company. As he walked, he made a strange variety of ticking and clicking noises with his mouth, in response to which the dogs all came quite close to him, and trotted as if called to Heel. He whistled a curious tune and at once, as if summoned by their Maker, a great flurry of yellow Finches came and flew about his Head, with one almost Roosting inside the bald spot atop of it. After another whistle, they flew off, but then came a parade of Cats such as I have never seen before or since. These animals, I knew well enough even then, are most reluctant to come to anyone's call, or hurry upon an errand other than their own — and yet here were at least a half-dozen of them, trotting along like *Kittens* after their Mother! As this strange confabulation of creatures drew near us, we could make out still one more Member of the Assembly — a white Mouse peeped at us from the man's Pocket!

At last this strange party came to a Halt, and we instantly did the same. The man smiled, bowed deeply, and began to address us in the most mellifluous and enchanting of tones. I could not understand his Speech, if by that one means the Words, but in the

Tone of his Discourse there was such ease that I stood as if some strange Spell had been cast upon me. I was overcome by a desire to Please this man, who was so *Pleasant* in himself, and who had such admirable Affinities with the Animal world. Sam, for his part, looked as dazed as I felt, and could hardly think how to reply. At length, he did speak, and it was simply to lay out our situation as Plainly as could be, communicating with words and signs our Weariness, the length of our Journey, and our great hunger. To this, the man replied with laughter, and further light words. At a gesture, he dismissed his entire entourage, which straightway dispersed about the grounds, and beckoned us within his singular Abode.

I had not, at that time, been inside any Human Dwelling place, and so had nothing with which to compare the Wonders I beheld. Never the less, I was fairly Confident that no other House was made as His was, with an eye to both the Human and Animal worlds. There were, at the level of my Eye, a number of doors and archways, perfectly accommodating the average Quadruped, and I passed by similarly sized Alcoves, in which were placed bright Cushions and bowls of Food and *Water.* At the same time, at the Human altitude, there were Tables laden with fruit and fresh vegetables, Couches of rich silk with Velvet draperies, and numerous benches upholstered with soft cloth and scattered with *Pillows.* The whole place seemed to have been built with such Double business in mind, and all in such a sensible and Complete manner, that it would have seemed Absurd to imagine any *Other.*

Our host invited us into an inner Chamber, where a fine repast was laid out for us both, as though we had been Expected. For Sam there was a steaming bowl of Porridge, a variety of Fruits and a large wedge of Cheese; for me, there was a large copper Basin, filled with the most tender grains and Vegetables, which had been cooked in Barley-water. I did not see any Meat upon the table that day, nor on any Other, so although our Host was too gracious to mention it, I was certain that its Absence was due to his devotion to his Animals, and his Abhorrence of the Idea of *Eating* any of them. After our feast, we were led to a pair of Beds — Sam's furnished with a soft mattress and a cotton Coverlet, mine quite heaped with fresh clean Straw. I doubt that either of us ever enjoyed such a Sleep as we did that day, for our weariness was as Profound as the relief we felt in discovering such a Friend. We must have slept the evening and night together, for we woke at Dawn with the Cock's-crow, and found again an ample Meal set before us. Our Host was not present — doubtless his many Duties on the estate did not permit him to Wait upon our rising, but he would make his appearance shortly. Which indeed he did, within a little less than an hour; he once again bowed to us both, and directed Sam to a washroom where a large pail of warm water, with ample Soap and Towels, awaited him.

On emerging from his Bath, my Benefactor was restored to his former self, shiny and Pink; Mr Bisset had also provided him fresh *Cloathes* from his own Closet, and although they hung quite Loosely upon his small Frame, Sam did not seem to mind. We were again welcomed, with words of the *Kindest* tone, and I understood from Sam that we were to have the Run of the Place, and amuse ourselves as we saw Fit. We did so quite happily, discovering on our Peregrinations much more about the Place that surprised us, and not a little that *Amazed*. The outbuildings had, like the house, been outfitted for any sort of Animal or Man; the only exception being the Barn, which was, as with the more common sort, designed entirely on the scale of Horses; the only difference being that their Stalls had no doors, nor was there any sign of Bits, Reins, saddles or Stirrups, such as would ordinarily be employed. I did, on closer inspection, discover a Whip — but as it was quite old and dusty, and gave the appearance of having long lain idle, I thought nothing of it.

The grounds were beautifully kept, though we could find no sign of any other Persons on the Property. There had, apparently, been a Mrs Bisset at some point, for a portrait of her with her husband had a Prominent place in the Parlour, but if she were still *Extant,* there was no sign of her presence. Once or twice a Week, a wagon arrived with such Provisions as were required, other than those which the Farm itself produced, and twice each day, without fail, we sat down to a fine meal which was set out for us. We had our own dining-table, as did the cats, and also the Dogs, upon which was set every delicacy that each Animal might have desired — with the exception, as I have said, of Meat of any sort. Mr Bisset had developed a sort of concentrated Food, in the form of Pellets of compressed vegetable matter, which were *Flavoured* in such a manner that all seemed to find them Palatable. Even the Mouse had his own sort of concentrated food, but he alone was fed by *Hand,* as he rarely left his Master's Pocket, save at night when he retired to a little suite of rooms that had been made for him in the manner of a child's *Doll's House.* This was placed on a high shelf, though whether to keep him Safe from the many Felines in the house, or simply because it was at a convenient Height for leaping in and out of pockets, I could not tell.

The only other activity we could discern in the home took place each afternoon in what must have been the former Drawing-room. The Cats were often called to Attend, but what it was they did therein I could not tell, as the door was kept closed at all times. The one Glimpse I caught was of a pair of brightly coloured Stools, between which a length of Cord had been tied, though what use such an arrangement could be to the Cats I could not begin to *Imagine.* And yet, in that Sight, I sensed that some further Demand, some greater Expectation, was made of us, the Animal residents of Mr Bisset's Demesne, than simply to Live, and Frolic, and wander about his Grounds — indeed, that there was yet to be revealed some dread *Command* with which we all must Comply or else Forfeit the many accommodations made for us in this his *House.* This feeling, during all my first Time there, was very closely associated with these Doors, and I was quite convinced that, once they were to be Opened, all would be Revealed to me, for Better or for *Worse.*

And so one day it was. It began much like any other, in that a welcome *Meal* was all laid out upon Table and trough, such that both Sam and I were soon sated, and ready to set out upon our daily *Rounds* about the estate. We were accustomed to seeing Mr Bisset strolling upon the large stone *Patio* that adjoined his home, and there indeed he *Was,* but so strangely Dressed and Appointed that we scarce Knew him. He was attired in a complete suit, *cap-à-pie,* of Black silk, along with a Waistcoat of red *Satin,* a tall Hat of Beaver fur, and a great bow Tie of some checked material. He looked for all the world like a Showman in want of a Show, and indeed this appearance was to be borne out in a moment far more absolute than I was then capable of grasping. He strode into the Hall, and stood before the twin Doors of the occluded Room, then *Bowed,* most deeply, in my Direction. I did the same in Return, having many times observed such Formalities, and then stood in Awe as the Doors of Perception were most suddenly thrown *Ope,* revealing, no concatenation of Cats but rather this simple Tableau: the twenty-six letters of the *Alphabet,* and the eleven numerals from 0 to 10, which comprise the Alpha-numeric Range of these our *Numbers.* In that sight, I beheld at once the double path of my Destiny, for by these Means I might give Utterance to my *Will,* and yet with these same Characters Mr Bisset could express *His,* and by them I would — as I am even as I write the very words you see before you — henceforth be *Bound.*

5

In the time of the Spanish Inquisition — a History with which I later became Acquainted by these same means — it was customary, before Torturing those accused of Heresy, to show to them the *Instruments* of their Agony. Many were so overcome by the mere *Thought* of these implements being used upon them that they at once Confessed to whatever charges the Inquisitor might name, heedless of how by every Word they were thus Damned. Well I knew that Mr Bisset possessed the power of commanding Animals to do his will, but the *Means* by which he obtained this power were yet a Mystery. The charm of his voice, his pleasant outward demeanour, the food he prepared and set before us, these were surely the chief Rewards that he employed, but what were his *Punishments?* As these letters and numbers swirled before me, I Resolved, if it were Possible, never to discover what it was that my new Master would do if I did *not* follow his Commands. And, of course, that was what all the other Animals before me had doubtless done, out of the same Conviction I presently felt, that such a discovery must be as Terrible as the rewards were Pleasant — and that would have been Terrible indeed.

Our routine, which began that Day, never varied. Mr Bisset would point to a card upon which was written a letter or number. He would then Name this card, using several slight indications together: a motion with his eye to the proper card, a pattern of clicks (say, one click and two clucks), and then a third sign, which was a common Word in English. These words did not begin with, or in many cases even include, the letter in Question, but were the sort of words one could easily use in a sentence without drawing any special Attention to them. Words such as 'Presently' or 'Shall' or 'Receive' or 'Answer' — each of them a cue for a letter, such as J, O, H and N (which are in fact just the letters they represented). He would vary the signs he used, sometimes clicking quietly just under his breath, sometimes employing the words in a Sentence, such as 'Presently you shall receive your Answer.' At first the signs were always accompanied by his pointing out the correct letters on each card, after which I would approach the shelf on which they were laid, and pick up each in my Mouth, then drop it on a chalked square on the floor, in the order in which they were Demanded. Once I had perfectly memorised this routine, he would gradually withdraw his other Signs, employing his Eye only. It was remarkable to me that I nearly always Understood his intent, a Phenomenon I can only account for by Supposing that these oft-repeated Routines had established a sort of *Intuitive* understanding between us.

This whole system, I soon realised, was designed to enable him to carry on with whatever Patter he liked, all the while sending me a clear set of Signals as to the Cards I was to choose. If there was ever any doubt, a brief but imposing glance in the direction of the card wanted, was all that was needed. Which it was unlikely ever to be, for we rehearsed for at least an Hour every day, for the better part of three Months, at the end of which time I had so Completely attuned myself to this Procedure that I could perform it quite without Hesitation or even

Thought of any kind. Indeed, whenever Sam chanced to use one of the words that were my signals, I was placed in great Distress, until I could relieve it by fetching the proper letter. By this means, quite by accident, I found that I was able to communicate with Sam, and he with me; he quickly made up a set of smaller cards by hand-writing letters and numbers on squares of pasteboard and, by practice, managed to learn the same Signals my master had Designated for them. Sam's delight in our Discovery was unbounded, and each Night after Mr Bisset had gone to Rest, he would run me through my Letters.

All this, of course, while it gave me great facility in Spelling any word upon Command, made me no more enlightened about their Sound or Meaning than a Blind man who had learnt his way among the Shelves of a Library; a great *Feast* of the World's knowledge was set before me, and yet I could not partake of so much as a single Crumb. My Benefactor at once set to work to correct what he regarded as a most unkind oversight by demonstrating for me the Sounds of each letter and word, and how they came together to make human *Speech.* He would speak, then spell his meanings, and follow this by spelling out a

Word in silence, and have me puzzle out the whole. Well I recall the very first word I learned, and it will come as no surprise to you, my Patient *Reader,* that this word was S-A-M.

We had to be careful, of course, that I did not vary from my Routine with Mr Bisset, or give him any *Idea* that I in fact had come to understand the Letters I had previously arranged in ignorance. And yet it did Amuse me to see the sorts of things he had me Spell — given *Names* were most common among them (John, James, Susan, Alice, Charles and so forth, in great variety), along with words that were meant to answer some simple question, such as Y-E-S, N-O, P-E-R-H-A-P-S and N-E-V-E-R. There could be no more doubt that I was intended for a Show, and a show whose chief Attraction would be to display my seeming-knowledge of the Names of those in the Audience, and my seeming-answers to their *Questions.*

I must admit that, despite the monotonous nature of these exercises, I took a better Conceit of Myself from this time, imagining the *Fame* of being such a Notable performer — but then, of course, I thought back to my Prize at the Fair, and how it had been given to my Owner rather than to Me. After all, would it be Man or the *Pig* who would most surprise the Crowd?

At the same time, with Sam as my tutor, I was embarking on a Course of Study that, though Elementary for any Human child, was *Extraordinary* for a Pig. Among the books in the Study in Mr Bisset's house, Sam found a tattered copy of the Fables of *Aesop,* in the Translation made by Samuel Croxall for the use of the eldest *Son* of Viscount Sunbury, who had been at the time just Five years of Age. It featured small wood-cuts at the Head of each tale, which were of great help in my Understanding their Sense, and since the Characters within were all represented as Animals, I readily learnt their names. It struck me at once that these so-called Animals were far more Foolish in their nature than any in my Acquaintance, but I soon realised they were but Figures, standing in for the Folly of *Man* — and, as Men are very foolish, the stories were many, and a great source of Pleasure. I should note here that our usual Practice was for Sam to read the tale aloud, directing me to the New or harder words as he did so, and repeating them until he was sure I had their Sense. By this means, we proceeded far more Quickly than if, as Human children do, I had to manage to *Speak* before I could Read.

Before long, we could see the signs that Mr Bisset was at last Preparing to set his Show before the Public. By turns, the Cats, the Dogs, Finches, Monkeys, a Hare and, finally a group of Turkeys were all led into the Practice room and marched through their routines at double-time. All had been instructed along similar lines to those I had experienced, with Repetition being the *Key*, and a series of soft, sharp signals the *Prod* for them to go through their Paces. The doors were now left open, and I was able to see the Monkeys dance, walk a tight-rope, and play a Barrel-organ, observe the Cats at play upon their Dulcimers and regard the poor Hare beating a drum with a Mallet attached to his Tail. The only group of Animals that had no training as such was the *Turkeys*, and here I must confess that Mr Bisset hit upon an expedient that did him little Justice, and would have greatly Dimmed the applause had anyone Known of it: he simply placed them in a small wire enclosure, the floor of which was heated to the point where it became uncomfortable to *Stand*, and the efforts of these poor Birds to avoid scalding their Feet produced the 'Country Dance' advertised.

Each day of the week that followed, we

were visited by a constant stream of trades-men with their vans, who delivered specially built cases for the Animals, loads of fresh Straw, canvas dividers and drop-scenes, and stacks of handbills printed on brightly col-oured paper. A large wagon, hitherto cov-ered and hidden in a far corner of the Barn, was brought forth, and carefully painted and refurbished. A much-*Splattered* man with an immense bucket of brushes appeared one morning; although a carriage-painter by trade, he fancied himself a far worthier art-ist than that, and approached the task at Hand with the gusto of a minor *Michelan-gelo.* On each side of the wagon, he painted several oval cartouches depicting scenes of Mr Bisset's performing Animals; I am somewhat Ashamed to say that I was *De-lighted* to find Myself the subject of the central, and largest of these. 'THE RE-MARKABLE SAPIENT PIG,' he wrote in letters of red edged with gold, and had I the ability not merely to Read but to *Speak,* I am certain I could have given him the Shock of a Life-time, by quoting those very words back to him. The next day, the word was given out — or the Sense of it, at any rate — that we were to Leave on the Mor-row, and once again, I wondered at the capacities of the World, and at the Strange and Singular path my way through it had so far *Taken*, and appeared very likely to take Again.

6

My next Progress through the World was far more Comfortable than my Last. Rather than being jostled about in utter darkness in a gloomy enclosure filled with foetid Straw, I was ensconced in a lovely wooden Case, so spacious one might almost call it a *Room,* fitted with a small Trough of clear water and a stack of fresh Carrots, with clean grass for my Bed and a view of the Road before me. This Case was cleverly fitted with a wooden Rim about the bottom, so that it held close to, and stayed secure atop, the other Crates beneath and beside it, all of which were secured with heavy leather Straps. The Horses trotted along in their curious Manner, directed by Mr Bisset without the use of any Whip or other device such as a coach-driver would employ, but only by his Voice, and in a manner so efficient that he never needed to Shout, but that the Horses would speed, or slow, or turn, or halt, in such a Natural manner that it seemed almost as though the idea was their *Own,* and not an act of Obedience to another.

Our Tour, for so it was to be, commenced in the smaller Market towns along the road that led from Manchester to *Liverpool,* passing through Warrington, Newton-le-Willows, Wigan and *Prescot.* By this Progress, or so I inferred, Mr Bisset hoped we might work the Rough edges off our Act in smaller venues, where audiences were more forgiving, before we unveiled our Production to the more Discriminating show-goers of the larger Towns and *Cities.* There was, I discovered, a regular Calendar-full of Charter fairs in each of these towns, held for time out of mind on certain set dates, typically the *Feast-day* of some local Saint. Apparently these Saints must all have been Patrons of *Commerce,* for they very conveniently arranged that their Festivals would follow in perfect sequence, so that a travelling showman, such as Mr Bisset, could attend each one of them in Sequence, without having to backtrack or sit idly, from the middle of *May* to the end of June.

Being relative Upstarts in the show-world,

we were generally relegated to the less frequented part of the *Pitch,* as a fairground is known, while more experienced showmen had the advantage of the best Ground, where the greater number of people would Pass. Never the less, I believe we readily overcame this disadvantage, due in large part to Mr Bisset's canny nature, and Sam's limitless energy. The Horses were our chief Ambassadors: outfitted with colourful Caparisons advertising our Show, they processed through the fair, pausing every so often to perform a series of Tricks. They were so well trained that, at a single Word, they would execute their full routine, as well for Sam as for their Master. Sam had only to learn the bit of patter that accompanied their act, and to lead them from place to place. By the time they returned to their Stalls, they had each brought a dozen or more fair-goers in their *Train,* and as every showman knows, having a Crowd is the best way to attract a larger one.

The opening routines with the dogs and monkeys were, to my mind, of a very Ordinary sort, but they were colourfully arranged, with each calculated to be just slightly more impressive than the last. The final scene, where one of the monkeys rode upon the back of a Dog, which executed a series of Leaps while the second monkey played a Barrel-organ, excited Universal shouts of pleasure, especially from the Children present. This was followed by the 'Cat Opera' in which a line of three Felines sat on silken cushions and struck at Dulcimers, all the while seeming very earnestly to read the Sheet-music set before them. At the same time, a series of Tom-cats would come a-caterwauling, yowling along with the music in a very tuneful manner — for Cats, at least. This opera then gave way to a brief Circus, in which cats rode a Barrel down a Rope, climbed a pole and sprang into a Net, and batted a great Wicker ball around a Ring. The Hare then beat upon the Drum with his Tail, while the Turkeys executed their 'Country Dance'; it required only a Modicum of Imagination to suppose that they actually moved to this *Music,* rather than leaping about to avoid burning their Feet.

All this was but a Prelude to my Appearance, which at first gave me a considerable fit of Anxiety. A performer is fortunate, I have since felt, if he struts upon the Stage only in the opening Act, like the guards of Elsinore in *Hamlet:* they have no one to follow, but all else must *Follow* them. Whereas, if one's Cue comes late upon the Bill, one must follow, and seem to *Exceed,* every Act that has come before. On my very first performance, I was most Reluctant to emerge from my Compartment, so much so that Mr Bisset rapped upon the Enclosure with his Cane, which sent me scurrying forth quite abruptly, and to much Laughter on the part of the Crowd. Happily, I soon recovered my *Composure,* and turned my mind entirely to the Task at hand, for which Mr Bisset was an admirable Guide. He had taken the Precaution of asking those who wished their Questions addressed by the wonderful Sapient Pig, to fill in cards with their names and their questions written upon them (if they *Could* not write, then Sam would take down their Particulars). Mr Bisset held these cards in his hand quite Openly, for of course it did not occur to anyone that he had any means of Communicating their contents to me. He would shuffle them up a bit — in fact, making sure that there were not two persons named 'John' or similarly common names as 'Tom' and 'Tim' as these would risk, however slightly, the audience catching on to his Signals. He varied the words he chose quite astutely, and occasionally would use his Shoe to scuff out the code for some of the letters in Taps, such that neither his Utterances nor his Demeanour appeared to offer any *Clew* as to the right answers.

There was a Hush, always, as I picked out the letters and numbers, and a great Cry of amazement when I spelt out just the answer. Besides getting the names, the Questions were all fairly Common: young Maids wanted to know if they would be married, and how many Children they would have, and would they have a lovely Home; Boys wanted me to guess their Age, and never complained if I Added to the Figure, while *Men* — who rarely participated, unless at the Insistence of their Wives — asked about only the most practical sorts of things, such as what price Apples would bring at Market this year, or what Horse they should wager upon at the *Races*. And my Master, since he made it his business to know a great deal about exactly such matters, was always able to give me a serviceable Reply, and when a Guess had to be made, one that pleased the Querent. At the end of my performance, I was to make a little Bow, and spell out 'G-O-O-D-B-Y-E', which always led to a great round of Applause, and a great take at the Nobbins (which is what we showfolk call the Money that is dropped in as a *Hat* is Passed).

We did a very good business indeed at

these Fairs, and by the time we arrived at the town of Prescot, we had taken in nearly a hundred *Pounds,* and Mr Bisset gave it out to Sam that we might consider carrying on to Liverpool, where he had a Friend who was the Proprietor of a *Garden,* said to be a veritable *Vauxhall* in Miniature, where we might draw far larger Crowds. There was only one Difficulty with this Plan, and that was the matter of Licences. The Magistrates in those days were often simply Men of the Town, of some Age and Dignity, whose usual purview was small disputes over Property, or minor civil offenders such as Disturbers of the *Peace.* When the time came each year for the Fair, they quite naturally extracted a Fee from all who would exhibit there. The fee was a standard one — amounts of five pounds or thereabouts were common — but the Magistrate was quite free to Increase it, for any arbitrary Reason, or, should the mood take him, to *deny* a Licence, even when a man was quite Ready to pay for it. Agricultural exhibitors, and vendors of food, were passed through quite Routinely, but as showmen we often faced a much more lengthy, and sometimes capricious, line of *Questioning.* Was the show harmful to public Morals in any way? Were the Animals treated in a

Humane manner? Was there any Trick or *Deception* by which the poor honest fairgoer was to be taken for his hard-earned money? We sometimes had to run through our whole routine for the Magistrate's benefit, and he and his Men might demand to see, and Inspect, any part of our Apparatus for signs of trickery.

Nearly all of the time, we were eventually allowed to put on our Show, though we were often assessed a higher Rate, to reimburse the Town for the trouble of examining us, or to stand surety against any later Discovery of deceit. Mr Bisset was a charming man, although I must say his power to charm *Magistrates* was as nothing before his gift with Animals. And this, as it happened, was precisely the Issue with *Liverpool,* as the Lord Mayor there, who was in charge of licences, was widely known to be especially Hostile to showmen. Never the less, with a ready venue, and the promise of great *Profit,* we hazarded the Journey, and the next day arrived in the little hamlet of *Wavertree.* From here, it would be but a short journey on foot into the City, and we could at least make Enquiry, to 'test the waters', as humans say, and see whether our *Hopes* might be given something to Feed upon. In the mean-time, our Bodies, at least, were well watered and fed, as we were lodged at Green Bank, near Mossley Hill, where an acquaintance of Mr Bisset kept a small dairy farm. Sam remained with me, thankfully, for I should not have liked to be left with Strangers, and we waited anxiously to see what the Result of our Master's enquiries might be.

It was late that night when he returned, and his Mood was darker than I had ever known it. The Lord Mayor's secretary had kept him waiting the better part of the Afternoon, and when at last he was Admitted, had given him only a very brief and *Dismissive* interview. Mr Bisset had exerted all his power, and with the assistance of some Friends of his in the City, had persuaded him to reconsider, but only to this extent: he must examine the Pig in question, without any interference, and all alone — nothing else would do! — and if at last he were satisfied that there was no Deception, he would consider granting permission for its Exhibition. Our Master was, of course, gravely Troubled at this, for he believed that without his Presence, and his Signals, I would be unable to Demonstrate my intelligence, and all would be Ruined. Of course Sam and I knew better, but we could not, even at this juncture, bring ourselves to Disclose to Mr Bisset my true Knowledge of Letters. We feared either that it would Break his Spirit, by making it seem that he was no longer *Needed,* or cause him to fly into a Rage at this betrayal of his *Secrets.* Never the less, Sam at least persuaded him that he should come along; perhaps the Lord Mayor would not mind if a young boy, said merely to be the pig's keeper, stayed by him.

This thought so delighted Mr Bisset that he at once agreed, and proposed that, in a single night, he would train Sam with at least a perfunctory set of signals, so that he could, if permitted, transmit them to me in His Lordship's presence. Sam, of course, already knew them all, but went along with the ruse, as being the easiest Solution to both his and Mr Bisset's *Predicament,* and of course, so did I. We ran through the signals for 'YES' and 'NO' and even risked 'MAYBE', which, at five letters, was as far as our Master ventured to trust us. By means of these three replies, he hoped, we might be able to Convince His Lordship that, under the strictest measures, there was neither Fraud nor Deceit in this our Show, but that it was in fact an innocent, and indeed an *Instructive,* demonstration of the Native Wit of the *Porcine* race. It was quite late by the time we had completed our exercises, and as we were due in Town at ten the next Morning, we all retired at once, Mr Bisset to his Friend's cottage, and Sam and myself — as had become our habit — to a common bed of *Straw* in the back of the Wagon. And there we slept, deeply and Soundly, as we had never slept before, and woke *Refreshed,* as though we had drunk the waters of Elysium, and wandered the hills of *Paradise.*

Our journey into Liverpool was not a Long one, for although we travelled entirely by *Foot,* it did not consume more than half an Hour. That noted City was not quite so Built up in those days as it has since become, save along the *Quays,* where a great deal of Business was done; the greater number of the Buildings were of a Low sort, and the lanes not much different from those of the smaller Towns, save that they were more Numerous and *Crowded.* We shortly arrived at the Town *Hall,* an impressive stone edifice with tall vaulted Windows, and a Roman sort of Portico. We were informed that it had once been topped by a square Tower, which had recently been *Dismantled,* in order that a round dome could take its Place, but at the time of our Visit, this work was *Incomplete,* and the roof quite Flat. Our

Appearance on the Steps caused quite a commotion, for although a Pig in the streets of Liverpool was quite beneath anyone's *Notice,* a Pig on the Steps of the Town *Hall* was cause of Clamour and Outcry. Never was I more *Offended,* or taken Aback at the human Prejudice of feeling, than I was when two tall men dressed in the Livery of the *City,* came upon me with great Brooms, as though to *Sweep* me off their stairs!

Fortunately, at just this Moment, the Lord Mayor's secretary came forward, and motioned us back down the stairs, explaining that our *Examination* was to take place in a builder's Yard on the opposite Corner of the Square. Here, with the blank brick faces of the neighbouring Buildings for our Enclosure, we were met by the Lord Mayor, a red-cheeked, huffing man by the name of James *Blackburn.* He did not exhibit any Sympathy of any kind — which hardly surprised me — but more than that, he seemed to possess a sort of Anti-Feeling that was so pronounced as to be almost a *Feeling.* My master was dismissed at once, though to his great Relief, Sam was permitted to remain. Mr Blackburn retained only his Secretary, who took his station at a little Table in the corner of the Yard, quill in Hand, to transcribe the *Proceedings.*

'Ah, so this is the Celebrated "sapient" Pig, eh? Is that correct?'

No one else seeming ready to answer, Sam ventured a 'Yes, sir.'

'And of what does his Sapience consist, eh? Can you tell me how many Ounces in a Gill? Name the most prosperous port in the *Antilles?* Tell what disguise Achilles wore when he was hiding amongst the women in the Palace of *Lycomedes?* Hey! Speak your Wisdom, you learned *Swine,* or for ever hold your *Peace!*'

To this I could not, at first, conceive of any Answer, so dire and Strong were my feelings. But then Sam, who knew a good deal more about these strange *Queries* than I, began his Signals — as subtly, if not more so, than our *Master* used to. First, he signalled the number *Five,* which I quickly pickt out from the *Numbers* that were among our Cards. So much for the ounces in a *Gill!* I thought. And then, at his direction, and by Eyes only, he had me pick out P-U-E-R-T-O and R-I-C-O. Last, he had me spell out this phrase: 'D-R-E-S-S-E-D A-S A G-I-R-L.'

Throughout my Performance, the Lord Mayor looked upon me most Intently, his eyes *Widening* answer by answer. By the last phrase, his jaw quite literally Dropt, such

that one could almost Hear it go *Slack* —
here was a Man astonished, as they used to
say, Turned to a very *Stone!* It was a long,
full minute before he could muster up his
Reply, even as his Secretary sat Poised with
his Pen to take it *Down,* and it was this:
'Hah! I dare say we have here a Pig better
schooled than Half the Aldermen of the *City!*
Ho! By God, Wilkinson, here there be *Wonders!* Give this Pig a *Licence,* and tell his
Man that he is certainly the Lesser of the
Two!' Thus saying, half Laughing and half
Reproaching himself for his Doubts, Mr
James Blackburn the Younger stept Out
from the Yard, leaving his Secretary to
scribble us up a Licence, for which I was
most heartily *Proud* — for This I had done
by Myself, with my Benefactor's help only.
God save the city of Liverpool! To this day,
it remains the one place in the World where
I can say I proved my Self by my *Self* —
and for that I shall ever be *Grateful.*

Our Licence at last secured, we returned to
our lodgings at Green Bank, and shortly
removed to the Juggler Street *Market,* which
was at that time a common place for shows
of all Kinds. It consisted merely of a Wid-
ened portion of the main Street, part of
which was taken up by a group of *Stalls,*

with the rest left open for a varied array of Entertainments. The cost for erecting our Show here was steep, being £5 6s., but Mr Bisset had great Plans, and considered the fee a mere Pittance. Here we would perform but a Reduced version of our regular programme, and give out handbills and discounted Tickets for our upcoming Engagement at his friend's place, which was called Ranelagh *Gardens.* I must Confess that, having some time later attended the Establishment of that Name in *Chelsea,* it Bore no *Resemblance* to Gardens whatsoever. For, despite their grand Name, these 'Gardens' would in fact be better described as a Yard adjoining a Tavern. In its midst there stood a modest Amphitheatre, with wooden benches and a Stage that could accommodate a few Players (though certainly not a full Orchestra). In a manner that was, at best, a dim *Echo* of its London namesake, each evening commenced with a Concert, followed by a few tawdry Entertainments, and concluded with Fireworks. Our appearance there, to my Mind, would Raise both the Custom and *Reputation* of the place by a considerable Measure, besides bringing a very handsome *Profit* to Ourselves.

And so indeed it came to pass. For the first week, our performance was preceded by a musical *soirée,* featuring the talents of a certain Mr Morgan upon the *Violin,* and the vocalisations of a Mrs Ellis, but the Interest was so Plainly in our *Favour,* that the proprietor decided to give us the Top billing — upon which Morgan and Ellis promptly quit the show, being most Unwilling, they said, to follow a *Pig* upon the programme. Their departure was Lamented by *None,* and Mr Bisset quickly expanded our Act, adding a Routine we had practised, whereby I would 'Tell' the time after examining a pocket Watch provided by a member of the Audience, as well as a Clairvoyant Act, in which I seemed to read Minds. Of this particular portion of the show, out of professional Pride, I will not disclose the *Secret* — but those who are Privy to similar Acts performed by *Humans,* will easily be able to infer how I managed to fit the same Bill. It is still Remarkable to me that there are more people willing to credit a Pig with *Extraordinary* powers than with the most Ordinary ones, such as the understanding of the Rudiments of *Language.*

The Gardens were packed to their Limit every Evening, and even though the proprietor hired carpenters to put in additional *Stalls* on either side of the benches, the crowd spilled out on to the Grass, with people vying for the best *View,* and jostling one another in their anxiety to behold this new Wonder. We had a run of nine weeks, with almost no decline in Attendance, and drew our show to a Conclusion more for the sake of our own Rest than for any slackening in our Business. The last night was the most crowded of all, and at the end of our Performance, we were met by the Lord *Mayor* and a Committee of Prominent Citizens, who presented us with the Liberty of the Town, and claimed pride of place as the First city in which the Learned Pig had made his *Public* reputation.

It was by this time quite late in the Year, and the Season for performances out-of-doors was quickly drawing to a Close. We had one other Prospect that Mr Bisset had contemplated, which was to take ship from Liverpool to Dublin, where we might manage a booking in an indoor Theatre or Lecture-hall. He had already corresponded with a number of possible venues, sending along the latest clippings from the Press as evidence of our Warm reception. The most notable of these was Astley's Amphitheatre, a dependent *House* of its Parent Chapter in *London,* which did an enormous trade in Equestrian shows, with a Variety of other Acts between. As the Premier establishment of its Kind, its Rates were far higher than any we had yet Commanded; the least expensive Seats cost a Shilling, with private Boxes running from 10s. 6d. to £2 11s. More might be made in a single Night there than we had earned in our entire time in Liverpool, and Mr Bisset was quite keen to secure an Engagement.

We waited a further Week, the Weather being quite Dismal and *Wet,* and almost had decided to go Home, when a letter arrived via the Dublin Packet. We were offered a two-week stand at *Astley's,* with a most generous Guarantee against receipts; should Attendance be better than contracted, we would gain a Percentage of the sales of Tickets. Mr Bisset was beside himself, and Sam's mind was quite *Overtaken* with thoughts of Dublin. And yet, for myself, I must in Truth declare that I had begun to Weary of the life of a *Performer,* and secretly Hoped that I might enjoy some months Away from the Stage, or perhaps even *Retire* with my Laurels intact. Never the less, seeing my Benefactor's heart was so much Set upon the *Journey,* I undertook to accompany him *Freely* and put aside my Doubts, trusting that our Success *There* would mean a longer, quieter time *After.*

The next morning, as we went to board

the Packet, I encountered the first of what, in retrospect, seem ill Omens. The Captain of our Vessel absolutely *Refused* to have any Animals above deck, however crated or Constrained; we must be in the *Hold*. No amount of Cajoling would change his mind, neither any *Sum* — and Mr Bisset made a most Generous offer, more than *Twice* the fare of a human Passenger — induce him to Budge so much as a Fraction. I was therefore hauled down Below by a pair of stout young Sailors, and my enclosure *Packed* with all the others, alongside a slatted crate of half-starved Cattle, and several boxes of laying *Hens*. It took some ingenuity, but Sam, of course, eventually managed to *Find* me and, though his Visits were brief, he brought me morsels of his own *Food,* and News from above Decks, such that I considered myself not much less Comfortable than I would have been Above. The crossing was a lengthy one, with an intervening Call at the Isle of *Man,* and it was very late indeed that I learnt — by Sam's shout — that the distant lights of Dublin could be seen.

As we drew up along the stone Quays of the River *Liffey,* I could hear the shouts of the *Stevedores* as they readied their ropes and nets, and before long I was at last restored to Fresh air. As I was hauled out on a Pallet, I caught my first Glimpse of that vast *City,* which was the dim outline of the Custom House, and behind it the lamp-lit streets of a bustling Metropolis. So here we were: at the peak of our Fame, doubtless soon to be the Talk of the *Town* — and yet, for some reason I could not *Fathom,* I felt nothing within my heart but a sort of cold, containing darkness that I could neither penetrate nor shake off.

8

Our Lodgings in Dublin were of the Best
sort imaginable, with my Master and Sam
in a suite of Rooms, with a door opening
right into the Inn-yard, a portion of which
had been fenced off for the accommodation
of myself and Mr Bisset's other Animal
companions. The very next morning, we
met with a Mr *Sweet,* who introduced
himself as the chief Trainer at Astley's, and
spent some time looking over the Horses.
They went through all their paces, but Mr
Sweet seemed strangely Displeased by their
performance, although he gave their Abilities his grudging Admiration. 'They may do
Tricks, sure, but these Horses aren't properly *Trained* — we'll have to keep them apart
from the others in the Ring,' he declared.
From what I could gather, his idea of training had a good deal to do with the use of a

Whip, and he considered Horses trained in any other Manner to be a great Hindrance to him as he could not rely upon their *Obedience* to his commands. He did not bother very much about the other Animals, but did take a good long look at *Me,* and I felt at once a sort of Chill in his regard. He would just as soon see me cut into *Rashers* as have me cut Capers on his Stage, I thought, but since there was said to be some *Money* in it, he snorted, turned, and strode alongside Mr Bisset into his rooms.

Sam told me later that there had been some quite Heated discussion between them as to the Order of the Acts, and their Placement upon the Bills. There was a great number of human and animal Performers, who together filled the stage at Astley's, and just as in Liverpool, few of them were willing to share their Billing with a *Pig.* Never the less, the Attraction having been such a success, I was to be given at least a *Place,* and a by-Line, stating that I had 'just arrived from France' (this was meant, I suppose, to lend a sort of Continental cachet to my Appearance), and that, having been examined by the foremost Academicians, I had been declared to be 'the greatest production of *Nature'* as well as 'The Chief Philosopher of the Swinish Race'. Now I will say that I did not mind these *Sobriquets* half so much as one might think, but that they were not *Honest,* gave me considerable Pause. For what kind of Establishment, I wondered, would put in print such claims, so Patently and demonstrably False to anyone of knowledge or *Means,* unless it were simply to deceive the Poorer sort, who had no Idea of 'France' save what they read in the *Papers?*

All the same, the Realisation that I was about to become a *Pig* of greater Note was reinforced the next Day when there arrived a Tailor who declared he had been Sent for by the *Proprietors.* He duly took my Measurements, just as he would for any Human client, and returned the next morning with a Waistcoat of fine red *Silk,* with a pattern of small Paisley leaves. This garment was so well Fitted, that it seemed almost as Natural to me as my own Skin, only so much more *Elegant,* that I could not resist strutting about in it, and to this day it remains my most *Prized* possession. Thusly attired, I was attended that same Afternoon by a Painter, who was preparing a number of large canvas Banners, to be hung about the place depicting my varied *Talents.* Finally, as if all these other fittings-up for *Fame* were not enough, I was visited by Mr Sweet's assistant, who gently Trimmed my Hoofs, then applied something described on its container as 'Carr & Martin's Hoof Liniment'. The process of Beautification was completed with an application of 'Black Jack Enamel', a sort of shoe-polish for Hoofs, which made them quite nearly as black and glossy as any piece of *Human* footwear. Had I the Ability, I should have almost wished to ask for a Mirror, in which I might Behold my new *Appearance,* but once the assistant was satisfied with his work, he Extinguished his lantern and left me in the dim light of the Inn-yard, where I could only Imagine it.

The next morning we went directly to the Amphitheatre after our Breakfast, where Rehearsals were already in progress. Each of the performers was established in a small, roped-in area to Practise while they awaited their *Cue,* and I was heartily Amazed at the variety of Oddities there *Displayed.* There was a troupe of Tight-rope walkers, led by a Monsieur Bussart, along with a Tumbler by the name of Monsieur *Redigé:* these were apparently the Artists in Residence of Astley's, and conducted themselves as though they *Owned* the place. In the next area there was a Signor *Scaglioni,* whose dancing *Dogs* were a sight to behold as they cavorted, leapt and executed neat pirouettes. Near them, an exceedingly thin young gentleman by the name of Herr *Hautknochen* stood rehearsing his Singing Duck routine, which consisted of a variety of Comic songs, at key points of which he would Squeeze his Duck, which quite understandably let forth a loud and melodious *Honk* in response. Last, there was a most remarkable Woman, who went by the name of Signora *Spagniola;* she was practising an Act that required her to Dance with two Swords tied to her Feet, along with two *Eggs* — which remained miraculously Unbroken — all the while balancing on her *Head* a pair of Flower-pots upon a Board!

Amidst all these Novelties, there was a large troupe of Horses and Trick-riders, who were the Mainstay of the Establishment. Their performances were apparently so *Frequent* that they scarcely required any Rehearsal, and so they mostly stood about, idly executing handstands and adjusting the colourful trappings of their *Mounts.* Mr Sweet was their Director, and the *Impresario* of the place; it was he who was responsible for the entire evening's programme, and who *Announced* each act as it was about to Appear. The word was given out that, whatever one did, one should not *Cross* him: he was known to drop an Act from his

Bills at the least offence. For him, there was not one of us — excepting the Horses, of course — which was not *Disposable;* the public came to see 'Astley's' and the name implied a certain Quality, a certain *Class* of Entertainment, which was far more Valuable to its proprietors than any mere *Pig,* or dog, or Duck and his Man.

We found our own place was to be at the end of the first part of the Bill, which was generally reserved for newcomers so that an element of *Surprise* would mitigate the risk of Disappointment. Mr Bisset, I believe, was somewhat forlorn to find that his own Cats, Dogs and Monkeys could have no place among the rest, but surely if he found Success with me, he might hope to displace the rival *Hautknochens* and *Scaglionis* of his trade. His foremost concern, however, was that our Show, modest though it was, not be Lost in the glare and vastness of this new Arena. Accordingly, he made a new set of Letters and Numbers on a much larger scale than the *Old,* so that they could easily be seen even in the galleries and cheap seats. These I found somewhat difficult to carry in my Mouth but, with some care, I managed to transport them without Mishap; my worst fear was of dropping one prematurely.

Mr Bisset himself had rented a new and far grander Suit, with a brand new silk *Topper,* and an enormous red velvet bow tie that to my mind stood poised Precariously on the edge of the *Comical.* I had seen a number of Acts in which Animals were dressed as *Clowns,* and could hardly think of anything more Degrading; it is bad enough for Humans to disguise their Folly in foolish *Dress,* but far worse for us, who have at least the dumb Grace of animal *Sincerity.* Never the less, Mr Bisset wore his Cravat with such style, and animated his Patter with such native *Dignity,* that I was reasonably confident he would be taken *Seriously.*

And so at last the moment of our Dublin début arrived. The Amphitheatre was filled to Capacity, though to what degree our Presence had anything to do with this, we could not say with any *Certainty.* The riding ring was freshly powdered with Sawdust, and bright stage-lights were Beamed upon it from a bank of lamps furnished with highly polished *Reflectors;* that the whole place did not go up in Flames was a wonder (and indeed, in later years, both this establishment and its London Parent were several times consumed by *Fire,* and each time Rebuilt). The thumping of the horses' hoofs

87

was conjoined with my own still faster Pulse, and the noise and lights made it seem an Impossible thing that a lowly *Pig* such as myself could Enter, and command the attention of the Crowd in so boisterous an *Arena.* The trick-riders completed their stunts, the Dancing dogs executed their Moves, and the celebrated singing Duck hit all his Notes — and now it was time for us to step forth into that Blaze of attention. Mr Sweet, summoning all the resonant force of his practised Stentorian voice, declared that 'the Performances of this Animal are so truly *Astonishing,* his Intelligence and Instinct so *Great,* that they appear to be the work of *Magic,* and his Sagacity leaves all who see him in a Maze of *Wonder* at this Extraordinary production of *Nature* — and so, *Mesdames and Messieurs,* may I present *TOBY,* the remarkable Sapient PIG!' And so we stept forth.

In the glare of the Lights, I could scarce see any of the Audience, but only the brightly illuminated portion of the *Ring* within which my familiar Letters and Numbers were set forth — and so, despite the Enormity of the Crowd, I proceeded about my Act just as I always did, with Deliberation and *Alacrity,* and my eye always on Mr Bisset. He himself seemed to take a few moments to find his Voice, so vast was the Enclosure; he stood blotting his brow with a silken Kerchief, and blinking a bit in the Glare. Never the less, after my first Trick — which was answering his own Question as to Where we were (this, with a bit of Business, was drawn out into Comic routine, with my first answering, H-E-R-E and when pressed again, D-U-B-L-I-N, and finally spelling out, A-S-T-L-E-Y-S) — the Audience quite *Roared* its Approval, and he at once Recovered his Bearing in the Warmth of their Applause. Next, I answered a variety of queries he put to me about History and *Philosophy,* which were all, of course, *Rehearsed,* followed by an Invitation to take any kind of Question from the Audience.

This part of our Act, as may be imagined, quite regularly brought out all the Wiscacres and *Drunkards* in Attendance, as they were always quite Keen to prove a Pig a *Fraud.* My Master knew them well, and had in hand a series of Rebuffs, which generally *Shamed* them into silence, but here we were first confronted by a lovely young Woman, who simply asked, How I had felt on being *Taken* from the usual course of a pig's Life, and obliged to *Work* for a Living. We had a stock answer, which was R-E-L-I-E-V-E-D, and that I speedily assembled. 'Relieved in what way?' persisted our *Querent*. And it was then, much to Mr Bisset's lasting amazement, that I took the occasion to Spell out an answer of my own: N-O-T T-O B-E E-A-T-E-N. Everyone was Delighted with this reply, at which both Mr Bisset and I took a Bow, but I noticed as he did so that he cast his Eye on me, and hurled at me a Look — though whether of Wonder, or Disapproval, I could not tell. We then carried on with the remainder of our Act, in which I told the Time, guessed people's names and *Ages,* and played a game of Cards, and each new performance drew fresh Applause and shouts. We had, it was apparent, quite won Over the Crowd at *Astley's,* and could have hoped for no better result than the general Adulation of that body — for whatever the proprietor's or the Public's views upon *Pigs,* there was no arguing with Success.

The next Morning, we were visited by a Newspaper man, who wished to work up a Piece on us for the *Freeman's Journal,* said to be the leading paper of the *City.* He was a jolly fellow, Mr Robinson by name, and not only interviewed Mr Bisset, but insisted on seeing me, and putting to me a variety of questions. From this latter interview, he learnt that I was from Salford, that I had previously appeared in *Liverpool,* that I was two Years, one Month and eleven Days of *Age,* and that I found the accommodations at the Inn most satisfactory. All this was indeed written up in the next Issue, which Sam obtained and brought to me for my Perusal; while, of course, I had always taken some pride in my Handbills, it was a new and very grand feeling to see myself named in a *Newspaper.* In the meantime, Mr Bisset was making his social calls, and receiving numerous demands for Private performances, every one of which he politely *Declined.* For indeed, as he said to Sam later, were he to Answer every one of these *Calls,* the wind would be quite taken out of the Sails of the public *Shows,* for it was only because our performances were Scarce that they were *Valuable.* It was not until quite late in the day that he and I found ourselves *Unattended,* and then he cast me a Look that I shall never Forget.

'Now listen here, Toby,' he declared. 'I don't know how you've done it, or who's put you up to this foolishness — though I have a fair guess! — but I'll not have you *Upstaging* me, not ever again! Man over *Pig,* that's how it has always *Been,* and how it must Be. A little learning is a dangerous thing, it's said, but Understand me now:

any more *Learning* of that sort will be a far greater *Danger* to you, so long as you're in my Keeping. Have a mind! I can always take you to *Market,* and trade you for another Pig who'll learn just as *Well.* There's money to be had, so long as an Educated Pig minds his *Lessons,* and his *Schoolmaster* — that's what people want to see — but no one will put down a *Farthing* to behold a Pig as its own master! Now you will Mind your *Letters,* and take your *Cue* from me, or I shall do away with you, quick as *Thought* — do you hear? You may make your way through the World however you like, but were it not for Me, you'd have no *Admirers* on this side of a Butcher's window! And as for that worthless, impudent *Boy,* it's he who put you up to this, I'll wager my faith! The ingrate! I'll not have him about, I tell you! There's room for only one Master in this room, and I'll tan his *Hide* who hinders me!'

This Discourse, which was delivered in an undertone of *Rage* unlike anything else I had heard from a Human mouth, in an Instant disabused me of what little faith I had in *Humanity.* I knew, as certainly as I know *Now,* that there are *Degrees* of Every thing, but to see Mr Bisset in this light cast a new sort of *Darkness* over my entire Career. A kind heart he had *Not;* it was all

92

for his Convenience, his Reputation, his *Pride* that he had trained me, and as to his avoidance of *Meat,* I was sure now that was only a *Feint* designed to Lull his Animal tenants into a False sense of *Security.* No man ever looked more ready to Slaughter and Eat his interlocutor on the spot than did Mr Bisset on that occasion. I reproached Myself — I should have seen his true *Character* before, should have trusted the Fear that I first felt on discovering his Demesne, and seeing his Working of it! But most of all, I felt a true *Horror* at the idea that my Benefactor, the only person upon whose *Goodness* I could rely *Absolutely,* was to be sundered from me. Such a thing must not be! But how I could prevent it, I could not at that time Imagine, so bleak and hopeless my *Situation* seemed.

We completed our run of two Weeks in *Dublin,* although after that first Night, I scarcely allowed them to Register upon my mind. They passed, instead, in a sort of a Blur, like a rapid series of Dissolving-views thrown upon the Wall by a Magic *Lantern.* Sam was, in fact, not immediately Dismissed, but forbidden to be Alone with me, and put to work for Mr Sweet at a variety of menial tasks that were, I am certain, *Designed* to keep him occupied, and unable to assist me. Indeed, I overheard some Talk between my two *Masters* that they might very well arrange for him to 'stay on', which would mean that our departure from Dublin would be my leave-taking of Sam. This thought, combined with the sense of both Fear and *Loathing* with which I now regarded Mr Bisset, kept me in a sort of cool *Terror* throughout these weeks; it was only by closing off my Mind to such thoughts, and focusing solely on my business with the Letters and the Numbers, that I managed to keep my *Wits.*

And after the last evening, when Mr Bisset was paid off, my worst fears, alas, came *True.* He was a Wealthy man now, with well over two hundred *Pounds* to his credit, and a bundle of Letters inviting him to engagements in dozens of Towns throughout Britain. He had Promoted himself to a new Frock *Coat,* and his *Cravat* was now all of Silk, as were his *Hose;* a gleaming pair of jet-black boots completed his outfit, and he looked every inch a Man of *Parts.* For myself, I retained not only my Waistcoat but a small *Medallion,* given me by one of the Ladies in attendance, in the shape of a red ribbon with a silver Oval. It was, in fact, she told me, a medal that one of her late *Paramours* had been given for his excellence in

Oratory, and she declared that I had a better Right to it than *He*. Never the less, I would have abandoned both of these idle Adornments, if only they could have purchased the continued company of my *Benefactor*, without whom I could hardly conceive of continuing in *Life*. I do believe that, had not Circumstances intervened, I would sooner have allowed my Master to sell me for my *Bacon* than ever again perform for him, whose cruelty in severing me from my lifelong Friend was *Unconscionable*.

That night Sam managed to come to me, having crept out of the rooms where the Stable-hands at Astley's were lodged, scaled a fence and run round to the Inn-yard where I was caged. Many were our tears, and they would have been matched by Cries as well, had we not known that any *Noise* would bring the Master's *Wrath* upon us. Sam swore repeatedly that he would not *Live* without me, and I the same to him, using the little cards he still kept in his Pocket. He had grown in the past few months — indeed, he now looked a strapping young *Lad* — but to me he was still the boy who had clung to that *Wagon* as it raced down rutted lanes and round sharp corners, the boy who had *Stayed* when anyone else would have simply Abandoned all Hope.

He remained with me almost until the Dawn, and left with the *Promise* that somehow, in spite of Sorrow, our ways would Cross again. Sam's last gift to me was my blue *Ribbon* from the Fair, which, much to my Surprise, he had retained all this time. He now pinned it upon my *Waistcoat,* gave me a final Embrace, and then was *Gone.*

9

Mr Bisset was up before the Sun the next Morning, directing the porters at the Inn on how to load up his Wagon. I was soon hefted up in my Enclosure and lashed to my neighbours with strong leather straps, as securely as any *Prisoner* in *Newgate.* From the talk I had heard, we were to take a Northern course, stopping in Drumcondra, Drogheda, Dundalk, Banbridge and, lastly, Belfast, these places constituting an impromptu *Irish* tour on our way back to England. Mr Bisset meant eventually to get to London, where the scales of Fame weighed the *Heaviest,* but he was loath to pass up any opportunity along the Way. From Belfast, we would take ship, returning by way of Liverpool, Chester, Stoke-on-Trent, Birmingham and *Northampton,* the old showman's circuit, before arriving in the great Metropolis where he had already secured a promise of a month-long engagement at Astley's principal establishment, adjacent to Westminster Bridge.

Our first day's journey was the shortest, being just over two miles. Our way led out through the City, across a narrow *Canal,* and past rough pastures and small farms into a small, closely packed *Village* of drab brick houses, which bore the name *Drumcondra.* There was an Inn, a small stone Church, and a brownish sort of village Green, to one side of which was the Market square where Mr Bisset planned to stage his Show — and yet a more Desolate spot, and more Uncongenial to Entertainment of any *Kind* would have been Difficult to imagine. The few people I could see looked to be nearly the same *Colour* as the grey-brown bricks of their homes, walking about in a sort of *Torpor,* as though they had no will of their own but awaited the Instruction or *Command* of another. The children there did not smile, and the Dogs looked hungry; it was a Weary town, and one in which, had we been Wise, we would never have *Tarried.*

Immune to the charms — or lack thereof — of this drab agglomeration of people and Buildings, Mr Bisset at once established himself at the *Inn.* He had been assured by the proprietor that the Accommodations were pleasant, and that the next day being a *Market* day, his Show would doubtless be well attended. Mr Bellows was the innkeeper's name; in his appearance he was as oily as a wax *Taper,* and certainly put forth an incandescent Glow of welcome that first evening. We were all accommodated in the best Manner, myself with the other Animals in the Yard, and my Master in the finest Room, which had a sort of *Loge* overlooking us. Fresh slops were our dinner, although, without Sam to keep me Company, these seemed a cold and lonely meal indeed. It was not long before Quiet reigned over us Animals, while the sound of Messrs Bisset and Bellows, with their clinking glasses and their Guffaws, carried on late into the night.

And so day dawned — grey and sullen — without a bird, or a beam of light to its name. True to the Innkeeper's word, there was the Bustle of a Market-day outside the window, but to behold these creatures as they went about their Business was a cheerless sight, for not one of them looked up to see their or any other portion of the Sky — keeping instead low and steady, much as garden Worms, who live in dread of the sudden descent of a Spade. We established ourselves at once on what seemed the best part of the Pitch and set about our usual Routines, but to our invitations there was no ready answer. 'Has anyone a question for the Learned Pig?' my Master asked. 'Come, come, now, let the curious among you speak! Any Query, upon any Matter?' But question came there none. Mr Bisset was obliged, as he rarely was, to concoct a Dialogue with Himself, chiefly concerning mundane matters such as the Weather and the Time of Day, to which I answered one damp pasteboard *Letter* at a time. By sunset, which came early, we were all too ready to quit that place, with very little to show for our Efforts, the Nobbins amounting to a mere 4*s.* 6*d.* — the lowest we had commanded since our stay in Warrington, the very first Town in which our Act had been tried.

That night at the Inn, I retired early, unwilling to long contemplate the Dread I felt within at any number of future Performances I would be obliged to make amidst the Habitants of this Irish *Limbo,* working for a Master whom I no longer considered a Man, but rather a *Beast* who had still other Beasts in Tow. Worse still, I now knew little of our Plans or Progress, as I was without the company of my dear Benefactor, who alone had provided me with any Intelligence of our Doings. I now found myself in the midst of a dark descent, without my only Friend and Guide; like a *Dante* suddenly robbed of his *Virgil,* I was at the Mercy of tormented spirits, crooked Paths and fearful Precipices, with no one to direct my steps. Never the less, I resolved that I would not fall into that darkest chasm of all, the pit of Despair! I told myself repeatedly that Sam would find me somehow, and rescue me from these Torments, and until then, I must be as Stoic as any *Philosopher,* accepting whatever came my way with patience and Fortitude.

Both these Virtues were shortly put to the Test, as our northward progress proved to be a dismal detour. It rained continually, until the roads were churned into twin Rivers of Mud, and we were frequently obliged to stop in order to navigate our way through some new and unexpected Mire. At *Drogheda,* the market was so sodden that we scarce drew any crowd at all, and afterwards Mr Bisset was laid up in Bed for a week, with Rheumatism in his back and legs. When at last we arrived in *Dundalk,* there was a slight break in the weather, long enough for my Master to recover his Health, and we had an exhibition for two nights at the Assembly Rooms there, adjacent to the Town Hall. Never the less, after the expense of renting the hall was accounted for, our takings remained but little, and it was difficult to call to Mind our late glorious career before the lively crowds at Astley's, as we now plied our trade before an audience that seemed to consist largely of dreary, disconsolate souls, too weighed down with Drudgery to partake in Enjoyment of any Kind.

Several days later, we came into the city of Belfast by way of Banbridge, and here at last we found a more Profitable Venue for our Exhibitions. The Place was originally the Cellar of some long-extinct Structure, which had lately been refitted as a sort of Theatre, and was popularly known as 'The Vaults'. The manager there, a Mr Atkins, was most attentive to my Master's requirements, and very nearly repapered every Wall in the town with handbills. He personally arranged to obtain a Licence from the Magistrate, with whom he seemed on most friendly terms, and decorated the hall and the entranceway with banners depicting me with my Waistcoat and medallions, and declaring me the favourite of the Crowned Heads of Europe (a falsity which, though it pained my *Conscience,* so pleased my Pride that I found I could not complain about it).

Rooms were arranged for us at a nearby Hotel, and on the Evening of our performance, the street outside was filled with jugglers, Punch-and-Judy men, and other smaller entertainments, the better to entice the people to our own.

As a new Attraction this evening, we revived our *Clairvoyant* act, with which we had little bothered at our previous few shows, my Master averring that there was too little to read in Minds such as those possessed by the Inhabitants of Drumcondra or *Drogheda,* which were shaped by constant and laboursome Toil. In particular, we invited the *Ladies* to attend, experience having shown that they were more suggestible to our Routines, as well as more readily Impressed with the results. A modicum of Shrieking and Fainting does wonders for a show, my Master was wont to say, and there was some truth in this. And so, after our regular sequence of spellings-out of where we were, who we were, and answers to the shouted Queries of this or that Gentleman at the back of the Hall (they were, as usual, loud, and drunk, and were thus served with Comic answers), Mr Bisset enquired of a small group of middle-aged women, who were seated by arrangement with the Proprietor in a small *Loge* quite near the stage, whether they would Approach and see whether the Sapient Pig could see their inmost thoughts.

The key to this act was that, well in advance of the invitation, my Master had secured some little information about each of the *Ladies* in question. This had, for a time, been Sam's job: he would present them with complimentary tickets to the very best Seats, and conduct them himself, all the while chatting merrily, and picking up sundry small details. Through this, and by using a series of seemingly innocent questions ('Will your husband be joining you tonight, Madam?'), he determined which were married, which widowed, the names of their children and countless other trifles, all of which he duly delivered to Mr Bisset. Then, well before the performance, we would go over the 'thoughts' we were to 'read', cueing them to each by the order in which my Master would ask them their questions. There was some little chance of variation, or of one of the subjects insisting on putting their own *Queries* to me, at which he trusted to his usual set of silent cues, or — and this only as a last resort — to my ability, which he now knew all too well, to answer on my own. This last he thought most risky, and forbade me to improvise, save upon a certain special Signal, and of course I was loath to incur his Displeasure.

The moment having arrived, three Ladies were shown to seats upon the Stage, amidst much crinkling of dresses and fluttering of fans; although they were all of a settled age — perhaps thirty, perhaps forty — they were as animated and exaggeratedly Demure as *Schoolgirls,* and cast their eyes at me as though they had never seen such a thing as a Pig in all their lives. The first two were easily handled. Number One, a widow, enquired whether I could tell the name of her deceased Husband, which of course I managed without any trouble, along with the particulars of his Trade, and identifying a Watch as his. Number Two, who was in fact the Wife of one of the Proprietor's near relations, was more than delighted to hear of her husband's merits, the Names of her Children, and even her pet *Cockatoo.* Number Three, I thought, might be some trouble: she was the quietest of the lot, and blushed — though whether with pleasure or embarrassment I could not say — at each of the answers we gave to the ladies before her. Her jaw seemed clenched with some determination, and her eyes glittered like little stones; she joined in neither the laughter nor the applause of her Companions. When at last her turn came, she blushed still more deeply, and for a long time appeared to be almost unable to *Speak,* though several lines of questioning were suggested to her.

At last, by a visible effort overcoming her trepidation, she burst forth.

'Is it really true that your Pig can read minds?' (This to Mr Bisset).

'Madam, I can assure you, he has done so on Hundreds of occasions, without Error, and without causing his subjects the least Distress of any Kind,' was his reply.

She grappled inwardly with this. 'Very well, then. I should like to know whether my Husband has been Faithful to me!'

This was impossible. In the absence of the Husband, it was quite unclear whose Mind I was supposed to read. And yet I could readily perceive — as could, I am sure, my Master — that the woman was completely convinced of her spouse's infidelity, and sought only to have her suspicions confirmed. Were we, then, to give a Positive answer, we would incur her wrath — she might well claim that our Clairvoyant act was a sham — and if we answered in the Negative, we would instantly offend her *Husband,* who would be none too pleased, and likely to condemn our Act even more vociferously. Mr Bisset glanced furtively among the Audience, but due to the subterranean nature of the dim-lit Hall, he could not quite make out whether there was any Husband in attendance. At last, he could defer no longer and gave me the Signal to answer freely. I readily spelt out: 'N-O.'

The audience immediately roared their reaction, with the women, and the more sober of the men, exclaiming against the Impropriety of such a question, while those at the rear of the hall laughed uproariously, cheered and whistled. For the Subject upon the Stage, at least, this Answer proved to be precisely the one she had hoped to hear: she tossed a small silk purse at me — which we later found to contain five Guineas in gold — and strode off the stage with a look of fierce Determination. Her two Companions, their moment of public fame now spoilt by this unexpected Breach of *Protocol,* loudly expressed their disapproval, and ran — or nearly ran — as fast as their crinolined figures could carry them, down the aisle and out of the door behind her. The hoots, the catcalls and the shouts continued to mount, and soon made such a veritable Cacophony of Noise that the unfortunate manager, Mr Atkins, could hardly make himself heard over the Din. We endeavoured mightily to continue our Act, but were met only with raucous jeers and cries of 'How 'bout you read *my* wife's mind?', 'Bloody knackers!' and 'Geroff!', such that we were shortly obliged to quit the Stage, and make a hasty exit via the back stairs.

Luckily — or so it then seemed — the alley in which we found ourselves was adjacent to the yard of the Inn at which we were lodged, such that Mr Bisset was able to return me to my Paddock and slip into his own rooms without attracting any further attention from the boisterous crowd, who had since moved out of the 'Vaults' and were milling about on the street, looking for any sort of Trouble they could find, or make. From where I was confined, I could see the light in my Master's chamber, and heard him in a heated discussion with Mr Atkins, after which he paced back and forth before the Window, muttering words I could not discern. As nearly as I could gather, the manager had declared that he had sustained great Damage to his furniture and equipment on account of our Show, and insisted that the cost must be deducted from our Take — and no argument of Mr Bisset's could persuade him to withdraw this *Demand*. Shortly after Mr Atkins had quit the room, I could see that my Master had ordered up a flagon of ale — a very unusual thing for him — and appeared to be drinking it down with great gusto.

Not long after this, I must have fallen asleep, for my next recollection was of being awakened by an enormous clatter, like the crashing of a table laden with dishes as it was knocked to the floor. There then came shouts and *Curses,* followed by a series of dull thwacks, such as a heavy stick might make were it struck against a sack of Grain. Then the Door that communicated with the Inn's back stairs was suddenly thrust Open, and I beheld the figure of Mr Bisset in his Dressing-gown, which I saw was darkly stained with *Blood.* Immediately after him came a tall *Figure,* clad in a double-breasted uniform of blue serge, wielding a night-stick.

'*Mountebank!* God damn you to Hell! Your sort of *Filth* will not be tolerated in this City!' shouted the figure.

'Mercy! Mercy! I have a *Licence* from the Magistrate!' replied my Master, raising his hands in an attempt to shield himself from further blows. 'Good sir, if you are, as you seem, a *Constable,* surely you will not see me so ill-used, I pray you, nor violate the *Peace* you are sworn to protect!'

'Mercy? I'll show you *Mercy,* you fifth-rate cheapjack Charlatan! You've ruined me, ruined my Wife, and made us the Laughing-stock of the entire city, you and that damned Pig! I'll not have it! Hear me! If you quit these Premises, and this *County,* no later than Noon on the *Morrow,* I will mercifully spare your life and *Property.* But if I find you Here, I swear by my *Oath,* I'll have you Flayed within an Inch of your Life, slice your damned Pig to *Ribbons,* and sell them in the Market for country Bacon! Your operatic cats shall Gut my *Fiddle,* and I'll hang your monkeys from the nearest Tree!'

At this, I heard from my Master a sound I had neither *Known* before, nor in my darkest dreams *Imagined* from any Creature, man or *Beast.* It was not merely a Sob, but a sort of Bellow, a complete, contracted *Obeisance,* which sent a horrid Chill throughout my *Being.* For who, and under what Circumstances, could make himself so *Low* to Another as this? Surely no Animal but *Man* could contrive it! Of course, I had regarded Mr Bisset in a very Dim light before this Moment, but I was *Repulsed* to Think that even the Worst of men could be put *Down* by another whose Scruples, if any, were even *Lower.* The words of *Goethe,* whose work has so enlivened my later days, express the Occasion perfectly:

Man calls it Reason — thence his Power's
  increased,
To be far beastlier than any Beast . . .

The Constable left my Master prostrate on
the ground and strode off at a brisk March,
as one who had done no more than his *Duty.*
I was at a loss as to how I might Respond
to this awful *Occurrence;* along with all the
other Animals, I was secured in my *Paddock* — but even if I was Freed, what could
I, a Pig, do? Would my testimony be heard
in *Court?* What weight would my account of
this singular act of *Brutality* carry against
that of a uniformed Officer of the *Law?* And
even in the most practical of matters, I was
unable to Console or Aid Mr Bisset, or sum-
mon a Doctor to his side. I would have done
all of these things, surely, if I only *Could* —
but, absent some *Human* intervention, I was
as powerless as any Mute and *Uneducated*
creature.

Fortunately, although I was the lone witness to this dreadful Attack, the Noise of it
had roused a number of people, including
the proprietor of the Inn, who soon came
out into the Yard and discovered the groan-
ing figure of Mr Bisset. Along with several

111

neighbours, he made an attempt to lift my Master to his feet; this failing, a narrow table was brought and used for a Pallet, on which the injured party was conveyed upstairs to his rooms. A few moments later, I saw a young Boy sent out to fetch a *Doctor,* returning shortly with a person I am sure was a member of that Profession as he wore a grey frock coat and carried a leathern bag, within which some variety of unseen Instruments could be heard rattling as he ran. Alas! Without Sam as my guide, I could gain no further intelligence of Mr Bisset's health until well into the next afternoon, when I heard a serving-girl remark about 'poor Mr Bisset'. That he was ill, but not dead, I could infer from the continued visitations of the Doctor, and the absence of any Undertaker or other gentleman in Mourning dress.

It was two more days before anyone came to attend to us *Animals,* other than the boy who brought our Slops, and this turned out to be Mr Atkins himself. He patted the horses, paused at the case within which the Monkeys were confined, and then approached me with some trepidation, which I could not at first understand. He looked in all directions, like *Midas*'s wife about to whisper her *Secret* to the bulrushes —

clearly he was afraid lest someone see him talking to a *Pig* — then spoke to me in a quiet undertone.

'Toby, my dear — *ehm* — your master, as you doubtless have sensed, has been very ill since he was attacked. We have, *ehm,* learnt something of his assailant — he appears, indeed, to be the *Husband* of the lady who questioned you upon the stage — and he has been brought in and charged. Such an unfortunate turn of events! The Doctor says there's hope, though! Mr Bisset is possessed of a remarkable constitution! This morning he was able to stand without assistance, and he insists that he will continue his Tour and make his way to *London.* It will be some time, though, before he will fully recover — until then, I'll be sure you're — *ehm* — comfortable. Yes, *ehm,* well, I do hope you're taking all this in — why, it *seems* as though you are, but *how* you do it passes my Understanding, I'm sure! Good day to you, then — *ehm* — I'm sure Mr Bisset will come to see you as soon as ever he can.'

This awkward discourse concluded, Mr Atkins glanced about him again, wiped his forehead with a handkerchief, and hurried back out of the gate. Another three days of 'comfortable' ignorance passed before, to my great surprise, Mr Bisset himself man-

113

aged, with some assistance, to make his way downstairs. Leaning on the innkeeper's arm, he made the rounds of the inn-yard, stopping last at me. How he looked! A large swelling rose above one eye, and bits of sticking-plaster still adhered to his neck; one of his hands was wrapped in a cotton bandage, and he was breathing heavily.

He and I had no need of words, really — in some way, we never had — but he stood a long while gazing upon me, and in his eyes I saw a strange, wistful look. He seemed to be casting his mind back over his career as a trainer of *Animals,* and wondering if perhaps the undertaking had been worth while. I looked for but could not detect his old mien of Command, though I am sure he could have Mustered it had he wished — but instead, his expression seemed almost *Apologetic.* And then I, with my little eye, sent back (as best I could) my forgiveness for his harsh words, and his separating Sam and me. After all, I reflected, he had been given his Desserts, and then some, by that *Constable,* who, although mistaking Private rage for Civic duty, had in some sense served as an agent of Justice, and a messenger of *Humility.* Mr Bisset seemed to take all this in, paused as if to speak, but merely smiled. Then, with a little wince of pain, he turned, and the innkeeper helped him back inside and up the stairs. We would, I now knew, soon be back upon our *Way.*

10

By the end of the week, Mr Bisset was able to walk unassisted, and declared that he was anxious to get on with his *Tour,* which had been so violently and unexpectedly interrupted. Never the less, he could no longer manage everything as he once had, being unable to lift or carry the many crates and props with which his wagon had to be loaded, and thus was obliged to take on an Assistant for this purpose. The man he hired, a narrow, wiry young fellow by the name of Edward Dobbs, seemed likely enough for the job — he was remarkably strong, and could carry a crate on each shoulder with no trouble at all — but his *Character* was far from reassuring. He was possessed of — or perhaps *by* — a pair of sharp, dark-brown eyes that were constantly darting about, as though they could find no

Rest on any thing, and this perpetual *Motion* extended into his limbs, his fingers and even to his Toes, when I could see them. He also had a sort of *Stutter* in his speech, of which he seemed deeply ashamed, and thus rarely spoke at all, unless it was absolutely unavoidable. Worst of all was his manner with us Animals: he seemed to regard us with a curious mixture of fear and *Contempt;* in all their wandering, his eyes never came to rest upon us, as if for them to do so would threaten his very being. How I wished that Sam could return to take his place — but Mr Bisset would not hear of it, saying we had but just enough time to manage the few Engagements he had arranged on our way to *London* without missing the Season there.

Our Journey commenced with the unavoidable crossing of the Irish *Sea,* which looked particularly cold and restless that day. Our conveyance was a modest Packet-boat, the *Maria Eliza,* whose small size put her quite at the mercy of the Waves, pitching this way and that, such that even the most seasoned travellers were soon hanging at the rails, or lurching towards the Heads, their countenances as grey as the sky. Mr Bisset, although he declared he had no Qualms about the voyage, soon found himself in a similar position, and hastily retired below Decks, where he remained for the duration. The crates containing 'livestock', as we were considered, were lashed to the deck in the open air, which gave us a commanding *View* of the voyage, at the expense of periodic dousings with salt-water whenever a wave crested over the rails. Alone among the passengers, Mr Edward Dobbs was entirely unaffected, which I attributed to the fact that he was in even more constant *Motion* than the sea.

At the Isle of Man, we changed boats to a much larger vessel, the *Duchess of Athol,* where Mr Bisset was able to obtain a private berth, and myself and the other Animals were secured well away from the rails, and provided with fresh straw. The sea had also grown somewhat calmer, with the result that most of us slept for the main part of the journey, awakening only at the sound of the ship's bell announcing that we were drawing near to Holyhead. We cleared the breakwater just as dusk was falling, and the great Lighthouse at the end of the pier was casting its brilliant beams over the Harbour. With the assistance of many capable Hands, we were able to unload our Wagon and all our gear, but the hour being late, we were only able to travel a very short distance down the main Road, stopping for the night at a modest Inn in the village of Four Mile Bridge, so named for its distance from Town, and its ancient crossing. The inn-yard was so small that my Master left us in our Crates atop the *Wagon,* and we at once fell asleep where we lay, being greatly wearied by our *Voyage.*

The next morning, we set out at daybreak on the road to Chester, which was yet about eighty miles distant. The sky was grey, the wind cold, and the rain constant, such that although we replaced our plain canvas cover with one of weather-cloth, we were soon all thoroughly chilled. Mr Bisset, though ensconced under a great heap of woollen rugs and blankets, was constantly shivering with the cold; at last he was obliged to leave the management of the horses to Mr Dobbs, and retreat to the interior of the wagon. The towns along our route, all of them with impossible Welsh names — Llanfairfechan, Llandudno and Llanddulas, to name but a few — sounded like something from *Gulliver's Travels,* and offered likewise the most Lilliputian sort of Accommodations — small rooms, small inn-yards and small beer. By the time we drew near once more to England, and to English names, they seemed almost *Shrunken* to our ears, and by the time we passed through Holywell, Northup and the aptly named village of *Mold* that very substance seemed to be growing upon our Selves, so dark and dank had our Habitation become. The idea of a metropolis of any Size, and lodgings more ample than a Thimble, was indeed the only *Hope* that kept us going.

We arrived in the vicinity of Chester on the afternoon of the fifth day of our Journey, and as if to signal the Blessing of heavens, the clouds parted and some rays of the Sun were briefly disclosed. Now, this city was unlike any other that I have seen before, or since, in that it was still defined by its ancient Wall, and very few dwellings stood without it. The old Gates of the City were like those of some medieval *Castle,* and I am reliably informed that the name of the place derives from the old Saxon word *Ceastre,* which has that very meaning. We found admirable lodgings at the *Blue-Bell* Inn, which was formed of two identical houses that had been joined together as one, behind which was an ample *Yard,* with fine Stables and, to my joy, an abundance of clean, dry *Straw.* Mr Bisset looked much the worse for our *Journey,* but on taking some warm Soup, he seemed more comfortable, and slept very soundly.

■ ■ ■ ■

The next morning, we met with a Mr Dawes, the representative of Messrs Banks and Ward, proprietors of the Theatre-Royal in Chester. He laid forth the requirements of his Employers: that the Act be both honest and *Amusing*, that we engaged to keep the stage clean and free of any dirty Straw or Manure, and that we fitted ourselves into the space of the *Entr'acte*, which was not to be longer than Ten Minutes. A Comedy was then being represented, Mrs Cowley's *More Ways Than One*, which Messrs Banks and Ward considered suitable, and as its Business had been only middling of late, they hoped that this new attraction on the bills might revive its sagging Fortunes. Mr Bisset assured him that it would, and invited him to see us at the *Inn*, where he would happily offer a demonstration of our Abilities, but Mr Dawes declined, declaring he had no time for such idle Rehearsals. 'Mind you,' he added, as he departed, 'this Engagement is for one night only. If you acquit yourself well, then we will consider extending it, but if you do not, then you may expect nothing more.'

We had apparently come a step down in

the world, and there was no way to ascend again but by our own Exertions. Mr Bisset declared that he welcomed the challenge; he was delighted to return to the Stage. He talked of new routines for us to prepare for our *London* début. And yet, for my part, I could take but little Pleasure in such things, nor feel so sanguine about our success. I feared for my Master, as it seemed to me that he was not yet recovered from his terrible *Beating,* nor yet from the chill he had endured on our late journey. His enthusiasm was as great as ever, but in many ways he seemed only the *Shadow* of the impresario he once had been. His hands were less steady, his eye less piercing, and his voice had a sort of Tremble to it, which it had never had before. That afternoon, as we practised with our Cards, I urged him to take some *Rest,* and delay the next leg of our journey, but he would hear nothing of it.

In the evening, we were escorted to a small box at the very edge of the Stage, from which we might the more speedily ascend when our Turn came round. One of the Players, a Mr Edwin, in costume for his role as Sir Marvell *Mushroom,* was appointed to give us our Cue, as he was to exit a moment before the rest of the Cast. That the

122

scene was to change from that of the Town to that of the *Country* was a perfect Excuse — our appearance would, as it were, set the stage for this Shift, even as the stage-hands were busily moving the props in and out. With his Periwig and feathered Cap, his face whitened and his wrinkled cheeks spotted with Red, Mr Edwin looked almost the part of a *Clown,* which — such that we had any anxieties about the too-high dignity of a Licensed *Theatre* — at once dissolved them. Indeed, our chiefest care was to remain still throughout the Overture — we were directly adjacent to the *Orchestra* — and the first acts.

As our moment drew near, I watched the Players go through their Moves, and reflected that they, too, lived but at the *Pleasure* of their Audience. What a strange whim it was, when People first put *People* upon a stage — and yet, this given, placing a *Pig* before them seemed perfectly sensible. Just as this thought was passing through my mind, there was Sir Marvell Mushroom, a bit breathless, beckoning us on to the Stage. We did our best to unfold ourselves after our long Confinement, and strode upon the stage to much laughter and applause — as much from *Surprise* as Anticipation, I am sure. In accord with my Master's instructions, a low Table had been placed before us, and my Cards laid on the floor beside it. And then we thought no more, but at once set to our well-practised routine.

'My lords, ladies, and Gentlemen,' Mr Bisset began, 'I come here before you this evening to present a *Wonder,* that men of both Universities, along with a Committee of Edinburgh *Physicians,* have been, despite their estimable Learning, utterly unable to explain! It has been said, but falsely so, that the Pig, of all *Animals,* is the most Intractable, stubborn, and *Lazy.* I shall here upon this Stage prove the wrongness of these common Sentiments, and more: that the *Pig,* when given the benefit of such an ordinary education as we suppose fitted for any Child, can at once apprehend the basic Tenets of our *Language,* and employ it with as much *Sense* — some would say More — than most *Human* pupils.'

My first few questions were always of the sort that could be answered with 'Yes' or 'No' and I had but to select the correct card of the two. This was calculated to be the sort of thing that would rouse the Audience's scepticism, and thus prepare the way for their greater Amazement, when I began to *Spell.* And, indeed, the effect, if anything, seemed far greater in this grand Theatre than it had in our more humble venues. Being asked what Place this was, and having replied at first, C-H-E-S-T-E-R, and, on further prompting, T-H-E-A-T-R-E R-O-Y-A-L, the great Intake of *Breath* upon the part of our Spectators, was quite literally Audible. There was but time for one Question from the Audience, and here we had to take care that it was answered with both Brevity and Alacrity, as our Ten Minutes were nearly up.

'Is there anyone who has a Question, upon any Subject, that may be briefly answered by my learned Companion? Come, come, surely there is one such!'

High up at the back of the Balcony, a woman, who seemed somehow familiar to me, stood and raised her kerchief in her hand and waved it with such grace that Mr Bisset immediately called upon her.

'Will you ask your Pig, sir, if he serves you Freely? Is he not upon some constraint, or fear of *Punishment,* lest he not trot out the correct Answer?'

'I shall let Toby speak for himself, Ma'am,' was my Master's reply. And so he did, and so I wrote: O-F M-Y O-W-N W-I-L-L.

This reply quite brought down the *House,* as there at once went up such a round of *Applause* as would gratify any Actor, along

125

with many shouts and cheers and demands that we continue our Performance. The noise only ceased when the Manager, Mr Dawes, came forth upon the Stage to declare that those who wished to address further question to the Sapient Pig could visit him in the *Stalls* when the Play was done. And, indeed, the moment the curtain fell upon the Human players that evening, there was a great Rush to Mr Bisset and myself to put to us more Questions, the which we did our best to Answer for the better part of an *Hour.* We were not too greatly surprised to discover that Ladies and Gentlemen of Quality sorted out much as did supposedly Lesser folk in that they asked either out of curiosity (this was mostly the Ladies) or a desire to find us out in some *Fraud* (this from the Gentlemen). We acquitted ourselves at all points. At last a rather portly fellow — whom we later discovered to be the chief Magistrate of that fair City — asked us when we could be seen again. My final answer, T-O-M-O-R-R-O-W, pleased all present, not the least of them Mr Dawes, who was anxious both to disperse the lingering Crowd, and to reassure both them and us of our continuing *Engagement.* We retired wearily yet happily to our lodgings, well satisfied with our evening's Work, and looking forward to the betterment of our mutual Fortunes on our way to what we hoped and expected would be our ultimate Triumph in *London.*

And yet it was never to be. That very night Mr Bisset suffered a sudden nervous collapse or *Apoplexy* such that — so I was told later — when the knock for breakfast came at his door, he was unable to make any answer. The housemaid, on entering, had such a fright at his Appearance that she dropped the platter, which at once brought the Innkeeper up from his rooms. Due to the curious construction of the *Inn,* with its two connected buildings and the stairs between, I was able to see and hear quite well the commotion that followed. Once again a Doctor was summoned, and on arriving hastily mounted the steps. Of his examination of the Patient, I could see nothing, but he emerged shaking his head, and had a very grave consultation with those assembled outside. I could hardly make out his words, catching only 'nothing' and 'I fear he may *not.'* And then, as I was about to regret once more the absence of my good Sam to bring me word as to Mr Bisset's condition, the Doctor himself with his assistant came directly to me.

'Well, Mr Toby,' said he, addressing me in a wholly natural manner, so rare among his kind, 'you'd best go and see your Master. I'm afraid he's not long for this world! And, as you would seem to be the only *Creature* who is on close terms with him, there being no other Family present, I'm afraid you'll have to do!'

With that, he and his man lifted me into my Case and carried me up the stairs into the very room where Mr Bisset lay. He looked very poorly indeed: his hair was all dishevelled, his skin a mottled red, and his eyes wide and blank — an indication, it seemed to me, that the chief *Tenant* of their shared Apartment was ready to remove, having left both Windows open. He had been, as it were, Propped up in his *Bed,* and his arms lay at his sides, no longer obedient to him whose mere *Look* had once commanded all. And yet there lingered yet some small portion of his Spirit, as his right hand, trembling, appeared to motion me near. The good Doctor opened the door of my crate, and I approached with hesitation, uncertain of what I should expect. And then my Master did a thing he never had in *Life,* which was to place his hand upon my Head. His lips quivered as he would Speak, but no words came forth, only a sort of shivering mumble.

The Doctor leant over, cupping his ear in his Hand and endeavouring to make out what words these were which trembled on the edge of speech. He frowned, listened again, and turned to me. 'Good-bye,' said he.

And with that, Mr Bisset's body seemed at once to relax and recede, as though the *String* that had stretched it taut upon its Frame had been undone, and he slid down into the bedcloathes, his last Exhalation of breath coming in the form of a drawn-out *Sigh.* The Doctor reached up and closed his Eyes, and everyone else cast theirs down, except me: transfixed by the sight, I could not turn away. I had never before beheld the *Death* of any being, although on many Occasions I had feared for my own, or that of other Creatures. That humans, and *Animals* as well, were all such expiring things, reaching our Date at some moment we could neither know nor postpone, came as a strange shock to my Awareness; like a mark of punctuation in the middle of a Sentence, it at once divided my own life into two Dependent *Clauses.* For knowing this, I knew myself, and was thence expelled for ever from my own Garden of Innocence. No *Angel* bearing a sword did I see, nor an

Angry *God* to escort me out; about me I had only a few of my fellow-exiles, none of them any Wiser than the other in the face of this, our strange and common *Fate.*

And yet, as I soon discovered, my immediate Destiny was in one most Significant manner divided from that of Men. Upon the death of Mr Bisset, I was no longer a Friend or Relation, but instantly transformed into a piece of *Property,* a Good, a *Chattel,* whose disposition would be consigned neither to an orphanage, nor to distant relatives, but rather to the auctioneer's *Hammer.* Along with the rest of what was referred to in the Bills as Mr Bisset's 'Menagerie', I was consigned to be sold on Saturday next, the proceeds to be given to his heirs and assigns, as soon as these should be located. I envied even Mr *Dobbs* who, released from his contract with his late unfortunate Employer, was at least free to seek his fortunes elsewhere.

Through the grace of the Innkeeper, we were permitted to remain on his Premises until the date fixed for our Auction. Never did I endure a more melancholy Period than this: without a Friend of any kind, and only the daily slops to mark the hours of my *Existence,* I was as alone as I had been as a young Pig in my sty. Nay, *more* alone — for then, at least, I enjoyed the companionship of *Pigs* and knew no other sort, whereas now I was no longer fitted for their Company, nor any more for that of Men. My greatest dread, indeed, was of being returned to those thought to be of 'my own kind', for among them all my Distinctions would be undone, and my Shame would be complete. I found only slightly less dreadful the prospect of being purchased by some other *Exhibitor,* for in the light of Mr Bisset's passing and my own impending *Sale,* such relations had taken a most *Material* cast, and seemed to me little more desirable than to be *Enslaved.* I knew not then, as I do now, the long history of the bondage of one race of humans to another, which so damned the name of Humanity to Either, but if I had, I can be sure, it would have been cold comfort indeed. For to see oneself in such a History is to gain only the Company of *Misery,* and not its end.

On the morning of this terrible turn, we were loaded for a final time upon our Master's old wagon, which had been covered with advertisements for the event, and driven about Town by Mr Dobbs. After making several long and jostling circuits of the *City,* we were at last brought round to the edge of the Market-square, where a pavilion had been erected, with a platform at its front, from which the auctioneer could address the bidders, and display us, his *Wares*. A strangely Festive atmosphere prevailed, with a great variety of vendors and street-sellers strolling amidst the crowds of townsfolk, and even a few Families of the better class all in their Sunday dress, with their *Children* in tow, attired as little Fac-similes of themselves. I had learnt enough history to know that a similarly celebratory air attended public Hangings at *Tyburn,* and doubtless the Burnings of *Heretics* too once brought forth their share of jongleurs and Jesters and sellers of meat-pies. I reflected on the whole vast history of Humans, so far as I knew it, and gave a snort of *Despair.* There was nothing else to say: it having been greatly tested over the course of my brief Existence, I had finally lost all *Faith* in the creatures I had come among.

As the 'celebrated sapient Pig', I was the great Feature of the whole affair, and thus all the other Animals were set to be sold before me. And so, the singing Cats with all their operatic Dress were knocked down for 10*s.* 6*d.,* and the Monkeys with their Barrel-organ fresh Transported by means of a *Guinea.* The Turkeys, now destined to have more than their Feet put to the Fire, brought only 3*s.*, while the Horses — whose many wondrous tricks and ability to Steer themselves were found *Liabilities* rather than Assets by the bidders — were sold at *Fifteen* for the pair. The dogs and the Hare were quickly dispatched at 10*s.* for the lot, the Finches delivered from one *Cage* to another for half-crown. Finally, my time on the Block arrived, and I was most Rudely handled, turned out of my crate on to the stage for all to gawp. Those in the crowd nearest me laughed and jeered and pointed, and one of the boys there pulled the Medal off my *Waistcoat,* and would have taken the garment itself had not the Auctioneer had at him with his Stick.

I had only just recovered from this Indignity when the sound of another scuffle reached my ears. At the edge of the pitch, there drew up a bold young man, riding a horse stained and splattered with the mud of travel. Much to the displeasure of those present, he was forcing his way through the Crowd, preceded by a remarkably vociferous boy who shouted, 'Make way! Make way!' as though his master were a Monarch, and the crowd merely his *Subjects.* Drawing near to the platform, but hidden to my view by the Columns that held up the tent, the tall Rider at last stopt and called out loudly and repeatedly in a voice that stirred my soul: 'This Auction must be stopt!'

The Auctioneer, unable to ignore or silence him, at last gave answer: 'And why must it be stopt? Who are you to make such a demand?'

'My name is Samuel Nicholson, and I am the business partner and rightful heir of Silas Bisset. I have here an order from Sir William Dunkinfield, High Sheriff of Cheshire, that these proceedings be stopt!'

This threw the whole assembly into chaos, as the Bidders loudly cried against any such judgment, with the Auctioneer alternately endeavouring to calm them, and to address this unwelcome *Newcomer*. But all this Noise was sweet *Music* to my ears, I having heard, against all hope, the Voice of my Benefactor, only grown a bit *deeper* as his Frame stretched taller. Finding that he could progress no further on his *Horse,* Sam dismounted and hurried to the side of the *Platform,* whence he leapt up in a single bound, and stood stoutly by my *Side.*

11

It would be impossible to describe with any fidelity to fact my Feelings on the great *Occasion* of this my reunion with my *Benefactor*. To be hurled down by Fortune is one thing, but to be hurled *Up* is another; indeed, I could scarcely credit my senses, and thought for a time that perhaps I had simply been struck unconscious, and that the whole affair was merely the creature of my own Fancy, a *Dream* in which — naturally enough — all my Hopes were to be fulfilled. And yet, as I did not Waken up, nor was this vision of happiness suddenly dispelled by one of Sorrow, I came at last to accept it as an actual Occurrence.

The Uproar caused by the sudden appearance of my Benefactor was enormous, and did not die down for a considerable time. The Bidders were the most offended that their Currency had obtained for them no Commodities, even as several of them had already Paid. After much cajoling, the Auctioneer at last agreed to refund their monies, and by this means our 'Menagerie' was almost completely reunited. I say 'almost' as, despite our considerable exertions, the purchaser of the Turkeys was nowhere to be found, and their career as Country Dancers had come to a sudden and unhappy Close. Never the less, given the painful means of producing this effect, it was not entirely unmerciful that their next encounter with suffering would likely be both Brief and Final.

Having done us the good Turn of refunding the money paid by the Bidders, the Auctioneer insisted that, in consequence of his Expenses, and the great Disappointment of losing his commission on these Sales, he be given some form of compensation. To this we agreed, and at my suggestion Sam paid him with the small purse of Guineas I had received at the commencement of all this Trouble, with the hope that this unasked-for *Fee* would settle our accounts with Fortune. Sam even managed, by advertising a modest Reward, to fetch back my Medallion, so I was very nearly restored to my original state, save for a few tears to my

Waistcoat. We now had to look to ourselves, and to what devices we could contrive, to make our way forward, and this Accounting was easily made: we had, besides ourselves, the Horses, the Dogs, the Cats, the Monkeys, the Finches, the Hare and the Wagon with all its crates and other appurtenances, all of Mr Bisset's stage properties, including his fine suit of Cloathes and silk hat, and (our debts to the Innkeeper having been paid) about twenty pounds in ready money. We were, in short, comfortable for the Moment, but without some steady source of *Income,* our resources would soon be depleted.

Sam, very greatly to his credit, was Reluctant at first to take up Mr Bisset's former trade, fearing that our having publicly to Stage ourselves as Master and Animal would have a deleterious effect upon our *Friendship,* which was so very dear to us Both. And although now, looking back, I will admit that his *Anxiety* was not entirely without substance, I argued then — and would argue *now* — that this was, after all, the best and indeed the *Only* thing to do. For having already, at the very commencement of our Relations, stept outside our Natural places and understandings, our entire career was founded upon a *Fracture,* and any attempt to mend it, would far more likely *End* it. Neither of us could ever be wholly at home among our own Kind, and the Stage was the only place where our Differences could truly be *Appreciated*.

We still had the addresses for the London bookings that Mr Bisset had arranged before his injury and illness, and Sam wrote to them in hopes that, by claiming the delay of 'unavoidable circumstances', we might possibly revive at least a few. In the meantime, we charted a Course that would take us through a series of solid market towns — studiously avoiding the larger cities — yet bring us by degrees closer to London. Thus we bent our way to Crewe, Stafford and Wolverhampton, and thence to Coventry by way of *Tamworth*. From there, our route would pass through Leamington Priors and Banbury, and next to Oxford where, Sam said with a laugh, we might gain some *Learning* to our Advantage. From there we were to follow the valley of the Thames (more or less), calling at South Weston, Beacon's Bottom, High Wycombe, Baker's Wood and Ealing, before making our final approach to the great *Metropolis*.

Our last necessity before leaving Chester was to make a visit to the Tailor's to have Mr Bisset's suit altered. It struck me strangely then, and still does now, to behold how one man's *Habiliments* may be re-tailored for Another, and how quickly — merely by way of pins and needles — this *Transformation* may be accomplished. When we returned the next day, Sam stept, quite literally, into our Master's old shoes — and his frock coat and cravat as well. He looked every inch the *Impresario,* and although it seemed strange to me to see him thus, I soon reflected that, since the audiences in the towns knew nothing of our previous Shows, they could hardly be surprised by the Substitution. This same Tailor very capably repaired my Waistcoat, adding in the process just a small amount of gold trim, an addition which I will confess was made entirely to suit my *Vanity.*

The Boy who had accompanied Sam on his journey to Chester — whose name was *Bannon* — remained with us, serving in the very role formerly occupied by my Benefactor, and he proved as bright and capable in that capacity as anyone of his years could be. He, too, had been employed by Mr Sweet at Astley's equestrian establishment in Dublin, and had been so cruelly treated there that Sam felt it his duty to bring him away with him. From them both I heard the tale of their Escape, which was not easily managed, for Mr Sweet — a man whose *Nature* so belied his Name as to make one Shudder — was the very strictest of task-masters. He had kept them constantly employed from dawn to dusk, locking them in a room adjoining the Stables each night. It was only through the kindness of a frequent patron of the place, a young man by the name of Barker, that they were finally able to make their way to freedom. Mr Barker brought them two suits of fine *Cloathes,* which they hurriedly donned in a darkened corner of the stables while he kept watch. And then, with a confidence that did him credit, he led them out of the front door as though they were his own *Children,* and thence they passed into the Dublin streets, unnoticed until it was far too late for Mr Sweet to make pursuit. Mr Barker paid their fare on the ferry to Holyhead, giving them ten Shillings each in ready money besides.

In speaking with the ferryman, they soon had intelligence of Mr Bisset's crossing — for who could forget a man with such a singular collection of Animals — and every one of them so well trained! — and picked up our trail to Chester. And then, as soon as he came upon one of the Bills for the Auction of 'Mr Bisset's Menagerie of Marvels', he at once knew to make haste.

But how, I asked, had he managed to obtain a Warrant from the High Sheriff of Chester? 'Ah, that was easy enough,' Sam declared. 'I never did have one! It was only an old bit of legal script I'd found, with the wax seal still dangling — see here!' He showed it to me. It was scrawled and composited in some legal hand, and I could make out not a word of it — which was, indeed, its very strength. The Auctioneer, even if he had been a lettered man — and few enough were in those parts — would never have been able to scry its meaning on his own. And so, just as Sam had calculated, he preferred settling his accounts in some other way than getting entangled in a mire of legalities. We all enjoyed a good laugh at his expense, though my own joy was (at best) half-hearted. For what if Sam's plan had failed? It made me pale as parchment to think on it.

The next morning, as the first of Phoebus's beams was peeping over the ancient walls of Chester, we set out upon our way. And a weary way it was to be, for in nearly every town upon our route we were obliged to rethread the needle of our plans, as the authorities of every place unravelled them. We could only perform on a market-day, and these varied greatly from town to town;

we could only perform within the market-square, or we could only perform *outside* it; we had to pass inspection of the Mayor, or the Bailiffs and Aldermen, or the Nuisance Authority, or the Examiner of Showmen and Van Dwellers. With each inspection, as a matter of course, came a Fee — sometimes as little as ten shillings, but often as great as five pounds, such that we were only rarely able to leave a town with any more money than we had had at the moment of our arrival, and frequently with less. What with lodging and food for our company, our twenty pounds were soon whittled down to twelve, to ten, to eight and to four. As we left Banbury for Oxford, we had but twelve Shillings to our name.

As for Audiences in these towns, I may say (I hope) without giving offence to any one place in Particular, that they were almost without exception raucous, disorderly and Rude. The Questions they posed to me were shouted and strewn with obscenities; the noise and the clatter of carts and street-sellers often quite overwhelmed my Benefactor, even when he declaimed at the very Top of his Voice. Small children poked me with carrots and twigs, threw rotted vegetables at the Cats and Monkeys, and took great delight in banging pots and pans to frighten the Horses. It was here, I believe, that our training by Mr Bisset proved its worth, for despite our Animal natures, we were not half so *Beastly* as the Humans in our midst. As for Sam, while these days were indeed a great Trial, they were also a sort of Crucible in which his baser Metals were by degrees burnt away, and his purer and Nobler substance Proofed against the corrosive contents of the human Stew. A showman's life, alas, is not all *Glory*, for beneath the glitter and the tinsel lies much heartache, and the open road is often strewn with Thorns. Never the less, it is not a life that few who have come to know it would willingly set aside, even if Easier and Quieter occupations were softly to offer their Alternatives. Perhaps if our road had come to an end *Prematurely,* and our appearance in Banbury had been our last, we might have felt a twinge of Regret, but it was a wise chance that brought us next to Oxford Town, where our mutual Fortunes were to take a strange turn that neither of us could have anticipated.

The city of Oxford possesses a distinction that, even before I laid eyes upon it, places it in a most Favourable light: it contains within it the name of an *Animal.* You may prate if you will of other such towns, and scribblers may speculate all they like as to the origins of Shrewsbury, Ramsgate, Swanage, or Sparrows *Green.* I have heard tell even of a town named Swindon, whose name is said to derive from a Saxon compound meaning 'the swine's hill'. But of all these fair places, there is none that remains so dear to me as Oxford, for it was there that my *Education,* having already proceeded as far as my Benefactor's little learning could take it, was so much further Developed that I could at last answer honestly to the Sobriquet of 'the Sapient Pig'.

Yet another — and, at the time, seemingly more significant — feature of the town of Oxford was St Giles's Fair, held from the first of September since the days of Queen Elizabeth, at a site adjacent to the Church of St *Giles,* where the Woodstock and Banbury Roads converged. It had taken diverse forms over the centuries, with sundry trades — the Gypsies with their heaps of China plates, the husbandmen of Oxfordshire with their livestock and cider, the toy-merchants with their dolls and miniature theatres — having precedence for sundry epochs, but with all being given at least *some* portion of the *Pitch.* The tariffs for this fair were not inconsiderable, and indeed our entire remaining purse of twelve shillings was thus forfeited — but the takings were likely to be far greater, for the officials were more welcoming than at other such Fairs, and its fame went far and wide. One hears now and then of the tensions between 'Town and Gown' in such places, but falling as it did within the Long *Vacation,* St Giles's Fair was unequivocally a *Town* affair, and thus all the better attended by the common folk for miles around.

We arrived the night before its commencement and, having paid our Tariff, found lodgings nearby at a small Inn adjacent to a cider-house known as the Spotted Cow, which suited us well. For, although Sam and Bannon were put up in a cramped room with three other men, it had a leaded-glass *Window* that overlooked the Inn-yard, such that they could keep a watchful Eye upon myself and the other *Animals.* The whole place was filled with exhibitors, many of whom regaled the crowd with previews of their Attractions; among them we saw a Gypsy dancer who played with great skill upon the Tambourine, a Juggler who managed five flaming Torches at once, and an operator of the *Lanterna Magica* who threw macabre pictures of Skellingtons and *Witches* upon the Walls. My Benefactor

145

fancied at first that he might give some Demonstration of my abilities, but thought the better of it after we narrowly escaped being *Trampled* by a passing party of Revellers carousing down the road. And so, rather than risking our necks in the crowded streets, we retired Early to our beds, that we might be the better *Rested* for our show.

We were very glad of it the next Morning, for we took our Breakfast while the other denizens of the Inn slept on, oblivious to the dawning of the day. We reached the pitch well before them and were able to lay claim to an excellent Position, in the midst of a patch of green near the foot of St. Giles's cemetery, just opposite Black *Hall.* Here we soon drew a considerable crowd, as we were very nearly the first outpost of the Fair that travellers from the North encountered. Indeed, on several occasions, the town officers had to come round and clear the road of carriages, many of which had pulled over so that their passengers could take in our Show. We now greatly expanded our Bills, as much for our own relief as to add Variety to the programme, and brought back some parts of our Act — such as the telling of time and the reading of minds, which had been abandoned in the course of our Provincial tour. The result was that on the second day of the Fair we were even better attended than on the First, and were near to Exhaustion with Encores.

It was near the end of this day, and thus of the Fair itself, that we were approached after one performance by an elderly gentleman, dressed in the plain frock coat and bands of a churchman. As he conversed, he seemed to be smiling quietly to himself, as though he knew, or suspected he knew, some secret about us. He particularly wished to be introduced to me, and his manner was surprisingly natural. He bowed slightly, then turned to my Benefactor, whispering something in his Ear. Poor Sam blushed a bit but, not wanting to give offence, nodded — evidently agreeing to something the man had proposed, after which he stept back, permitting the old gentleman to examine the pasteboard Letters employed in my Performances. The man did not, as did most, turn them over in his hand to look for tricks or ruses, but instead quickly selected a great handful of them, which he then turned and placed upon the ground. I approached with great Curiosity, and saw that he had from them formed this Sentence: I-S I-T T-R-U-E T-H-A-T Y-O-U C-A-N R-E-A-D A-S W-E-L-L. At which, quite without thinking about it, I dashed over and spelt out: Y-E-S. The old fellow then took out a book from his satchel, and laid it before me. I saw that it was a copy of *Ruddiman's Rudiments of the Latin Tongue,* a common school primer of the day. This time he did not spell, but asked me directly: 'Mr Toby, are you acquainted with the Latin language?'

To which, of course, I spelt out: N-O.

'Remarkable! Truly remarkable. To know the limits of one's learning is knowledge indeed, and as scarce — I dare say — among Humans as those of the *Porcine* race.' He then turned from me to Sam. 'Mr Nicholson, have you trained this pig?'

'I have, sir — well, my former master, Mr Bisset, gave him his first training, but I continued it. He taught him only to spell out words on command. I was the one as taught him to read, sir.'

'And you did not think it a Waste of learning to bestow it upon a pig?'

'Not at all, sir. Why, he had a liking for it from the start. Besides, what good is it, to pig or man, to spend one's whole career following commands in ignorance of their meaning or effect?'

'And to what purpose?'

'Why, for his enjoyment, sir. And mine.'

'And for the Exhibition of these talents to

the Public, you mean.'

'Well, yes. We all have to make a living, sir. But I never made reading part of the Act, sir. You see, if people had known that Toby could *read,* they'd have thought the *less* of him, odd as it seems. Better they think it a miracle, or some Trick they can't see through.'

'Yes. A showman must please the multitude. But what of yourself? What, more to the point, of Toby? Is there not a certain weariness in being bound to the Stage? Is there no more nectar to be had in other Pastures?'

'Why, surely there is, sir. But how should we have it? We have to pay our costs and our carriage. All must have their food, their straw and their shelter.'

'Yes, indeed. Well! You know the history of this University?'

'I know it's old, sir.'

'Yes — more than six hundred years old. But in its day, it was little more than such a pasture. The hunger and thirst for learning made men linger here, and to sustain themselves in that endeavour, they made arrangements for food and shelter. The spirit must lead the mind, and the mind the body, not the other way about.'

'I'm sure you're right, sir. But not all of

us have the ability to follow your good advice. *Stomach* calls, and the legs must needs follow, carrying mind and spirit with them — if you take my meaning, sir.'

At this the old gentleman let out a long and hearty laugh, and clapped Sam on his back, at last declaring, 'Well said, well said. I must be off now, but if you would do me the courtesy of calling upon me before you leave Oxford, I would very much like to receive you.'

To this Sam readily agreed, and was given an address upon a card. Having several more shows to do, we did not examine it until long after his departure, when we were gathered about a table in the yard of the Spotted Cow, myself having (for the occasion) a pint of Porter in a bowl set beside my customary meal of Oats. It read simply:

Dr William Adams
Pembroke College

This name meant nothing to us, though we assumed he was some Fellow or Tutor, and we decided to call upon him the next morning, as we were due to move on to the Salisbury Arms in the village of South Weston for a show the following day. It was only by chance that Sam mentioned the name to the Innkeeper, who at once let out a low whistle.

'Dr Adams! Don't you know? Why he's the Master of Pembroke, and a great man, for he was the Tutor of a still greater man.'

'And who would that be?'

'Why, Dr Johnson, of course! You know, he as wrote the *Dictionary,* and many another book besides.'

Which news amazed us both, for while we might know little of the doings of *Schollers* in their Gothic alcoves, it seemed that *everyone* knew of Dr Johnson. Indeed, among the modest shelf of books I could claim to my credit, his *Rasselas* was one of my favourites, and I had a neat little copy in *Duodecimo* among my personal Belongings.

Then came the Morning. We both trembled a little at being invited to join such august Company, but we could hardly refuse such a generous invitation. It proved to be but a short walk through the centre of the town to reach the College, and when we presented Dr Adams's card to the Porter, we were at once treated with unusual courtesy. Our horses and wagon were led into the Stables, and we were escorted across the inner yard to the Master's lodgings. We were met at the gate by Dr Adams himself, and he invited us to join him for tea and toast in his private garden. It was a somewhat awkward moment, despite — perhaps *because of* — his kindness; there had even been set down a copper basin for my own use at the foot of the table. Happily, my Benefactor had brought with him the smaller set of Cards, which we used for our own communications, and by means of these I was able (at least) to make answer for myself.

Inevitably, our talk soon came round to Dr Johnson. I expressed my admiration for the man, and brought forth my little copy of *Rasselas* as evidence. Dr Adams was delighted to behold it, and praised it as the most *moral* book the good Doctor had yet produced. He himself had encouraged his former pupil to compile a book of Prayers and Meditations, and had continually urged upon him the importance of *Religion* in a man's life. To these exhortations Dr Johnson had grown increasingly amenable, the more so as he had lately been quite ill, and could hear time's winged chariot drawing ever nearer. In fact, he was contemplating a final visit to Oxford, not knowing how much longer might be his allotment of life, and would be staying with Dr Adams — how astonished he would be to meet a *Pig* who had read his works! If we were to consider remaining, it would be most gratifying, and he would be delighted to *Introduce* us.

To these enticements my Benefactor replied with both gratitude and regret: our business in South Weston, and the other hamlets on the way to London, could not wait; it was in the nature of the showman's trade to make one's bookings in season, and to disappoint them would be ruinous. Dr Adams then enquired as to how much we generally made at one of these Venues, and Sam was forced to admit that, while we often took in as much as six or seven Pounds, our costs — when food and lodging were included — were often equal to or greater than that Sum.

'Well, Master Nicholson, I was about to propose that I compensate you for your time at least as well as your Shows would earn you — but now I see that to do so, I should have to *Take* rather than Give. But let me then give you more than your Custom, and closer to your Deserving. I can offer you a room here that lies at my disposal, with food and straw for Toby in our stables and meals for you and your boy in our Common Room. It would be for a week at most, for I have here a letter from Dr Johnson in which he purposes to arrive no later than the sixth instant.'

Seeing that Sam still hesitated, he leaned over, cupping his hand to his mouth as though to communicate some secret: 'And that is not all. I will give you, besides, two shillings a day for your trouble and, more, I will commence with *Toby* a programme of continuing his Education, as far as time and his capacity will permit. He shall begin with a course of Grammar, Rhetoric and Logic, and then proceed, if he so choose, on the long-appointed path to Arithmetic, Geometry, Music and Astronomy. We have here at the College many of the leading lights of these times, and he shall have the best Tutors in every subject, under my direct supervision. Come, come, what say you? Is it not a fair offer?'

There was little my Benefactor could say in response to so magnanimous a proposal, but he managed to offer one further query: 'What of me, then?'

'You shall be included in our tutorials. For you and Toby have known and worked alongside one another for so long, I could scarcely hope to separate you, even if that were my wish. No, both shall have the benefit of this course of study. What say you?'

We could both say only, 'YES' — and so it was agreed.

12

The week that followed, although spent in the quiet confines of Pembroke College and its grounds, was surely the most Eventful of my brief *Existence*. I was awakened each morning by the stable-keeper, who brought my oaten breakfast. At these meals I was joined every morning by Sam, and quite often by Dr Adams, who liked to begin his day early.

Michaelmas term being yet some weeks distant, the college's rooms were largely empty, although a number of the Fellows were in residence, and each morning Dr Adams invited one or two to join us. For our meetings, a stout wooden table was set up adjacent to the stables, and chairs brought out; I was given a large washing-bucket, which, overturned, made an ideal Platform, raising me to a height where I could see and be seen by all. Sam sat beside me and, using the shorthand we had perfected for the Stage, I could quite readily give answer to any of the many questions that were put to us — or, I should say, to *me*. I am pleased to recall that all those who came to the table as *Sceptics* departed from it convinced that, whatever other wonders the world might hold, a Sapient *Pig* must be counted among them.

Dr Adams, having proposed that he would model my Education on the Seven Liberal Arts, was as good as his Word, commencing with Grammar, in which he instructed me himself. I was amazed to find that Latin, far from being a language of especial Difficulty, was in fact easier than *English*, and much more consistent in its Spelling. In my early days of learning, I had been *Irked* to find that English employed the same letters, such as *gh* to convey such vastly different sounds as those of 'laugh', 'caught' and 'Ghent' — and so it was with much relief that I found the Latin *c* was always hard, that *ph* always made the sound *f*, and that its nouns were in every way Harmonious in terms of number, possession and all their other *Forms* (though these were, it was true, more numerous than in *English*). By the end of that first week, I was composing simple sentences, and had begun to read through the little volume of *Sententiæ Antiquæ* with which Dr Adams had provided me.

The anticipation that attended the arrival of Dr Johnson was enormous, and as the day drew nearer, my studies had to be suspended for a time, as the Master and all the Fellows were altogether *Consumed* with preparations. A large Banquet was to be held in the *Hall,* speeches and verses composed for the occasion, and a suite of rooms made ready for the great man and his entourage. I was greatly disappointed to learn that Mr Boswell was not to be among them, he and Johnson having been *Sundered* some time previous by a small misunderstanding grown *Large,* as so often happens among Humans. Never the less, the learned Doctor was to be accompanied by several other of his Friends, along with his personal Physician, and two men whose special job it was to carry the sedan chair he at times required, due to a great Swelling in his legs. According to his most recent letters to Dr Adams, he was feeling generally much Improved, without any fresh attacks of the *Dyspnoea* or pain of the Lungs with which he had previously been much afflicted.

The appointed day having arrived, I was brought from my usual place atop the washing-bucket by the stables to a new seat of honour in a corner of the Master's garden, where a low platform had been specially erected. My Benefactor was in attendance, and with him he brought the larger pasteboard letters we used for our Public performances. Dr Adams had, strategically, I believe, seated us at the very End of the receiving line, a place which, though least in Priority, was — like an exclamation point at the end of a sentence — greatest in *Emphasis*. My only fear was that the learned Doctor, whose health, though much improved, was still quite Fragile, might be forced by sheer Exhaustion to cut short his travails along this procession of obsequious Welcomers, and go directly to the Banquet within.

I need not have worried — for, indeed, the Great Man was disposed, his time of life having grown short just as his Reputation reached its Apex, to move along the line quite according to his Whims, passing over many a bow and scrape with an expression of Impatience, and so coming, very shortly after having snubbed the most junior of the Fellows, to our place, with Dr Adams at his side. He leaned forward, bracing himself with a stout walking-stick, and peered so directly at me that, were I a *Hu-*

man, I am sure I would have blushed. He then turned to his old master with a jovial look.

'Dr Adams, I suppose this must be Toby, the learned *Pig* of whom we have heard so much?'

'Indeed it is.'

He turned again to face me. 'I have a friend, Mr Toby — well, not exactly a friend in the usual sense, but more a jousting-partner of the pen, Miss Anna Seward. She tells me that, some year or so past, she saw you perform at Astley's in *Dublin,* and went so far as to pin a Medal — upon your Waistcoat! Now I have never known a pig to wear a waistcoat, nor can I conceive what use it could be to him — but now I understand there is a greater wonder still, that you are being instructed in the rudiments of *Grammar* by Dr Adams here.'

I bowed slightly, and quickly answered, Y-E-S.

'Then can you tell me, sir, what form the noun *litera* takes in the Dative Plural?'

Without hesitation, I spelt out: L-I-T-E-R-I-S.

'And the vocative plural?'

L-I-T-E-R-A-E.

Clearly impressed, he turned back to Dr Adams, and asked him how old I was, and how long I had pursued my studies.

'Toby is nearly three years old,' he replied. 'With me, his studies have been scarcely a week, but it was from Mr Nicholson here that he first learnt his letters.'

Sam blushed.

'Then,' replied the Doctor, his great face a-bloom with ruddy indignation, 'is the Pig a race unjustly calumniated! *Pig* has, it seems, not been wanting to *man,* but *man* to *pig.* Why, we hardly allow *time* for his education, killing him at a year old!'

One of the Fellows, who was loitering at Johnson's elbow, took this moment to give it as his view that considerable *Torture* must have been employed in order to make an animal so Stubborn into such a supple *Instrument* of learning. At this, the Doctor turned at once to my Benefactor.

'What means did you employ to teach your Pig? What threats? What tools? What commands?'

'None sir,' Sam replied. 'He first had his training from my late master, Mr Bisset, who never raised a hand to him, and as soon as I shewed him the Connection between Letters and *Sense,* he did the rest himself.'

'Remarkable! Why, this pig would have been killed in his first Year had he not been *educated,* and some would say protracted existence would be fair recompense for a considerable degree of *Torture*. My old master at Lichfield, the Reverend Hunter, was a Brute of a man, and if there was a path to Learning that could be trod without *Lashes,* he knew nothing of it. And yet here we have a kindness out of *Kind* — a boy whose gentle guidance brings so recalcitrant a creature to his Letters! Commendable, lad!'

Well satisfied with his encounter, Dr Johnson accepted the arm of Dr Adams and, with this help on his Left, and his stick upon his *Right,* managed the way up the stairs, down the corridor and into the Hall. We could see his Progress through the windows, and as soon as he was seated, Dr Adams sent for us, and we found that we, too, were to partake of the Banquet. Indeed, I was told later that it was at Dr Johnson's personal insistence that we were brought, and given seats quite near his, seats that many of the *Fellows* had coveted, as they jostled against one another to gain Proximity to their learned Guest. I believe this was the beginning of a general Resentment of my Position by many at the College, which later grew to such proportions that Dr Adams had constantly to contend with it. Never the less, for that one day at least, I felt that I had accomplished something so very *Notable* that it distinguished me for ever among all the Animals who have had the benefit of Lessons: I was invited to dinner by Dr Johnson.

The next day, the estimable Doctor was unwell again, having perhaps over-exerted himself at the Banquet in his honour. There is, it must be admitted at once, something tedious in *Praise,* the more so when it is the better Deserved. For if one has, in plain fact, accomplished great things, and presuming that one has not lost one's memory or other Faculties, this whole Business of praise is rather like an endless rehearsal of a Play based on one's own life. And, unless the Playwrights be men of uncommon gifts (and this is rare), the Play itself is *not* the thing, but rather a poor imitation or repetition of matters that one knows already, and yet one to which it is Impossible, without great breach of protocol, to *Object.* On and on it must go, through every last execrable verse upon the occasion of one's wonderful Visit, until the Visit itself be damned for the *Visitor.* Dr Johnson spent the next day in bed, attended by his Physician, who prescribed a regimen of *Squills* to keep the water down. By these means, he was by that evening much Improved, and the next day was able to accompany Dr Adams on a tour of Pembroke and some of the more notable sights of the University. Alas, although much disposed to ascend, he was defeated by the sixty-five steps to the Bodleian Library, an edifice of which it may be said that the path of Learning is at its *Steepest*. He departed the next morning with his Entourage, intending to visit Lichfield, where he wished to call upon Miss Seward.

Here I must insert a word about this magnificent Woman, whose virtues it quite exceeds my capacity adequately to praise. I had not known her name until Dr Johnson happened to mention the matter of the Medal, and upon Reflection, I realised that it was she, too, who had addressed me in Chester. On that latter occasion, I had not been able to linger, and had had no opportunity to Thank her in person; in the dim light of the Theatre, I had not been entirely certain of her *Identity*. That she was an acquaintance of Dr Johnson I would never have guessed, but now that I knew, I was most anxious to learn more of her. From Dr Adams I heard something of her history: she was, in fact, the granddaughter of Dr Johnson's late schoolmaster in Lichfield, the man whose stern manners and frequent employment of the Lash were so ill-remembered by his famous *Pupil.* She herself was a remarkable Scholler, and was said to have been able to recite passages from 'L'Allegro' when she was only Three. There was a sad chapter to her life as well: her sister Sarah, who had been engaged to Dr Johnson's stepson, had fallen ill and died on the very eve of their *Wedding,* much to the distress of both families.

The friendly animosity, and jovial contest that ran between Miss Seward and the learned Doctor seems to have begun soon after this time. Aside from caring for her father, she devoted herself almost entirely to literary composition, with an 'Elegy on the Death of Mr Garrick' among her early triumphs. Further elegiac verses upon the expirations of Major André and Captain Cook soon followed, and she had but lately completed her first novel, which was entitled *Louisa.* Throughout this period she had corresponded with, and was frequently called upon by, Dr Johnson who, though he was publicly dismissive of her ambitions, privately admired her intellect, and relished their literary and philosophical contests. Many were the subjects of their friendly debates, conducted almost entirely via the post; I was at a later date shown a number of these Letters, and earnestly expressed the wish that they might some day be published. In the weeks and months after Dr Johnson's departure, and with the melancholy news of his Death that came not long after, I often expressed a wish to visit Miss Seward, but was for that time detained by my Studies, which I was most anxious to pursue as long as Dr Adams would permit me.

That good man in every way endeavoured to Encourage me, and with his help I soon advanced, and embarked upon the reading of several of the more famous speeches of Cicero. Alas, though my Progress was very strong, my path lay strewn with numerous *Obstacles,* the majority of which were not of my own Making. For, as they say, *invidia gloriae comes:* a number of the Fellows of the College had taken umbrage at the *Attention* given me, and took to quoting passages from the College's Statutes; they claimed that the Master had no authority to admit me as a Pupil, or that if he did I should have to pay for my Tuition, and pass the requirements for Age and Good Character (the former of which I could hardly be expected to meet, as I was very far from my sixteenth year, and by no means sure to live so long, a single Pig year being equivalent to several

Human ones). To all these complaints, the Master patiently replied that as he himself was covering all my Expenditures out of his own resources, and would gladly avouch that both my Character and Capability were the equal of any lad of the requisite age, thus my position was entirely proper. Indeed, in the case of my Benefactor, he had already been admitted to the College and (having had the good fortune to be born on Guernsey) been elected the Bishop Morley's Scholler.

Never the less, a small group of Fellows continued their grumbling and complaints, and eventually wrote to the Chancellor, Lord North, with a bill against me. Happily, that eminent man was then engaged in a series of agonising political machinations with Pitt the Younger, which so preoccupied him that he could devote no attention to the matter, referring it to the Vice-Chancellor, a certain Reverend Mr Chapman. And that man, being on old and comfortable terms with Dr Adams, came one day to our Breakfast, and was so charmed by my abilities that he declared that, if I must go, then more than half of the Undergraduates must go with me as I was quite clearly their Equal, if not their *Better*. As a result, I was out of any immediate danger, being — or so I thought then — possessed as I was of the proverbial Friends in High Places.

And yet there I was soon to be proven mistaken, for the lack of any administrative relief of their Grievances did not, by any means, discourage my opponents; indeed, it *emboldened* them. It was just after the commencement of Hilary term that a number of undergraduates — encouraged, I am sure, by their Betters — came upon me under cover of the Night, shoved me into a Burlap sack, and made away with me to a nearby Public House, the Eagle and Child. There, they set me up upon a Platter, to which they tied me with a length of stout cord, and stuffed an Apple into my mouth, as though I were to be served up as their Dinner. *O tempora, o mores!* They then proceeded to exhaust themselves with Toasts, loudly proclaiming that the Establishment should be rechristened the Plover and the Pig, the Swan and the Swine, and other such names, and demanding that the proprietor set me up to Roast. That man, to my eternal Gratitude, refused their requests; knowing that they were from Pembroke, he had some inkling that I might be the celebrated Pig there resident, and did all he could to keep them preoccupied. So, while proclaiming the next round free of charge, he quietly sent round his boy to the Porter's Lodge; the porter fetched Dr Adams and that gentleman hurried to my Rescue.

I had, of course, no idea of this, and was as stunned as my captors when the Master strode through the doors in the midst of yet another round of boisterous toasts and taunts. When I look back upon it, despite the mortal terror I was in, I cannot help but laugh at the looks of utter dismay upon their ruddy faces — faces that, only a moment earlier, had been bedecked with grins and laughter. Their vital juices at once drained out of them as quick as beer from an overturned cup, and they made a drunken (and not very successful) attempt to rush out of the back door, which ended in a heap of twisted legs and flailing arms. Dr Adams himself was remarkably calm: he stood, walking-stick in hand, and fixed those young men with such a look that, one by one, they unfolded themselves and stood at attention. He asked them each to state their names (which, of course, he knew quite well already), then dismissed them with a word. He and the proprietor then removed the apple from my jaws and, with the greatest care and kindness, untied me and checked to see that I was unhurt. Having not my pasteboard cards about me, I could not express my Gratitude to them except with Looks, but these I am sure they Understood. At last, in the company of Dr Adams, I was escorted back to my bed in the stables, and given fresh water and oats to aid in my Recovery.

The lads who had absconded with me were given severe dressings-down, and their cases were referred to the University's Proctor; they all had to pay fines, and were abjured from any further such mischief on penalty of Expulsion. I was never so relieved in my Life, but it was clear to me at that moment that I could hardly expect to continue my studies under such circumstances. I had become a source of Diversion to the other students, and feared that there would surely be more such incidents; worse yet, I had become a distraction to my Benefactor, who was advancing so well in his own studies. I discussed the whole matter at great length with Dr Adams, who was, I am sure, grieved at the thought of losing me, whom he often called his 'second most famous pupil', and anxious that I need never return to the life of Show-Halls and street performances. At length, it was decided that, in such circumstances that — *aut disce aut discede* — once the regular

Term of the University was concluded, Sam and I should at last go to London. There, Dr Adams would take care that we were not made the subject of Vulgar displays for pecuniary compensation, but rather introduced to the members of Learned Societies, Athenaeums and other such Institutions, where my Learning would be continued, and I could demonstrate my abilities in an atmosphere of refinement and proper scientific *Enquiry.*

When the time came at last for us to depart, Dr Adams supplied me with letters of introduction, along with money sufficient to undertake our journey; the rest of the sum promised us he had caused to be deposited several weeks earlier in the hands of a London banker of his acquaintance, from whom we could draw on it as needed. Our wagon was cleaned and refurbished, the horses freshly groomed, and the whole load bedecked with banners and ribbons. Despite their earlier pranks, the young schollers of Pembroke turned out in great number and gave us a Roaring send-off, as though we had been a sort of School team. Dr Adams himself was the last to see us off, and I was surprised to see that he had tears in his eyes and Distraction in his Aspect — and he bore in his hands a copy of Dr

Johnson's *Dictionary* that the Great Man had personally inscribed to him. Against all my protests, he insisted I receive it as a gift, declaring: 'It will be of far greater service, and more perdurable value, in your possession than in mine. Take it! And, as you read, think on him who, for a time, accompanied you on the road of learning. *Docendo discimus, mi alme sus* — Good-bye, my friend!'

13

And so at last we finally turned our steps to *London,* which had — ever since our earliest days with Mr Bisset — been promised as our ultimate Destination. We had a journey of three or four days ahead of us, but as we had no anxieties for our upkeep, we kept a leisurely pace and took in such sights as presented themselves, in the manner of Gentleman travellers. Our first day's journey brought us to Tetsworth, a modest hamlet tucked away in the hills off the main road; we stayed there at a well-known establishment by the name of the Swan, whose proprietor was an old acquaintance of Dr Adams, and gave us very pleasant accommodations.

The next day brought us to High Wycombe, a more substantial market town whose chief feature was its Guildhall, an impressive structure of brick upheld by a series of open, arched colonnades. Here, we were to be the guests of the Earl of Shelburne, whose estate of Loakes House stood nearby, but His Lordship being detained by government business, we were welcomed instead by a friend of his, a gregarious little man by the name of Maurice Morgann. Mr Morgann had known Dr Johnson quite well, and indeed had stayed with him at Loakes House only a few years previous, at which time they had enjoyed a fierce debate over the merits of Shakespeare's Falstaff. The learned Doctor held that Falstaff was a fool and a knave, while Mr Morgann insisted that, fool though he sometimes seemed, the old knight's knavery was to a purpose, and formed a vital part of Prince Hal's education.

I was inclined to agree with this more kindly view, and indeed I could hardly have imagined a more well-disposed and jovial Host. We commiserated on the news of the death of Dr Johnson, but agreed with Mr Morgann when he declared that the great man's passing had been, in fashion with his life, most perfectly timed. He had known of his impending demise long enough to make his adieus and set his affairs in order, and knew that his Legacy was guaranteed; what better peace of mind could a man ask for? Mr Morgann himself was, he confessed, on his own way to Retirement; His Lordship's ministry being at an end, he had been gracious enough to confer upon him a generous Sinecure, placing him in charge of the Hackney Coach Office. He looked forward to setting his affairs in order, and perhaps taking up his new interest in Natural history. To that end, he asked whether I might mind submitting myself to an *Examination* that I might be entered in his Book, and to this I gladly consented.

He measured and weighed me most carefully (I was relieved to discover I was now eighteen stone and six pounds, only a modest loss of weight since my days as a Prize Pig), and interviewed me as to my life and background; here Sam was of great assistance, as I had to confess my earliest life to have been a period of absolute Ignorance.

We passed a most pleasant Evening, and the next morning enjoyed a large and hearty Breakfast. I was relieved to see that, the Cook having rather thoughtlessly prepared a large Sausage, Mr Morgann refused it, sending it back to the kitchen with the wry request that it be given 'a decent burial'; in its place he and we enjoyed oaten bread, accompanied by fresh milk and Cheese from

175

His Lordship's estates. Our next day's journey brought us still nearer to the outskirts of the Great Metropolis, passing through Uxbridge, whose high street was lined with solid buildings of timber, brick and stone. On the edge of the town, we came upon a large brick building of several storeys in height, which we were informed was a Factory for the making of *Chairs;* a Blacksmith's forge, a large Brewery and Malt-house stood immediately adjacent, each pumping out its differing *Fumes* into the Sky. The whole area seemed to be a veritable Hive of industry, and the people, bee-like, were so engaged with the buzz of their Business that the arrival of a wagon proclaiming a Learned Pig within was hardly worth a glance. In their dark monotony, these men reminded me of the poor folk of Drumcondra in Ireland, save that they seemed a more purposeful, hardened, sharp and Flint-like clan as they clanked along the cobbled streets in their hob-nailed boots; theirs was not a life of lassitude but of *Labour,* the sort of men whose motto might well be *absque labore nihil.*

We stayed that night at an Inn with the curious name of the Crown and Treaty; it was here, I was given to understand, that King Charles I had negotiated with the

176

leaders of the Parliamentary forces. Being conveniently situated to the highway, and equipped with large and well-run Stables, it was a favourite among coachmen; our stay there was pleasant enough, although I was constantly awakened through the night as tired horses were brought In, and fresh horses *Out,* it being the first and last stop for all travellers to and from London to points West and North. We were quite ready to leave the next morning, and took our Breakfast cold, and found that a heavy mist lay upon the road, which shrouded us from the Views of the approaching Metropolis, had there been any. All we could tell was that, the moment the way grew wider, it grew more crowded, as the throng and jostle of carts, horses, pedlars, costermongers, beggars, street-performers and errand-boys grew ever so much faster than the Street (for so it had now become) could manage to accommodate. It was a market-day, and this, I suppose, made things the worse for us, though the natives were so inured to such Bustle, that they had long ago ceased taking Notice of it, and carried on through the *Chaos* just as though it were the most ordinary thing in the world.

We soon found ourselves in the neighbourhood of Kensington, where the traffic grew (if possible) still denser, and we began to despair of making much further progress. Before long, we came upon a narrow Inn, with the name of the Half-Way House, though what points it stood between we did not know; in any case, Dr Adams had advised us explicitly to avoid it, as it was, in his opinion, a frequent resort of Highwaymen and pick-pockets. Instead, we battled our way eastwards, twisting through the narrow avenues of Piccadilly, where the ever-more-malodorous Mist took on the scents of urine, smoke and rotting vegetables. Finally, we came to Drury Lane, passing by the venerable portico of the Theatre Royal, and arrived at last at the hostelry Dr Adams had recommended, the White Hart Inn.

The proprietor, one Mr Lockyer, welcomed us most warmly, and brought us to a pair of rooms conveniently situated near to the Stables, such that Sam and I shared a communicating Door; these were the usual quarters of the Stablemaster, but had been vacated in our Favour. This singular kindness, our host informed us, was entirely due to Dr Adams, who had written some weeks in advance with a request with which he was very glad to Comply, the learned man having so often been a Guest of his. There was, we later learnt, more to their connection: Mr Lockyer's eldest son had been in large part supported by Dr Adams while an undergraduate, a favour his father had never forgotten.

We found the Inn to be most comfortable, and took our Supper in our rooms, while Sam and I looked over our remaining letters of Introduction, to see what our next step should be. Dr Adams had written, with great flourish, to Joseph Banks, the President of the Royal Society, whose offices were but a short distance away at Montagu House in Great Russell Street. We were a little abashed to call upon such a Luminary, but were assured he would receive us; the other letters were addressed to John Sheldon, a leading Anatomist, Richard Kirwan, the Chemist, and William Aiton, the Superintendent at Kew Botanical Gardens. I declared then and there that I would rather meet with Banks than with any of the others, having no desire as yet to be Autopsied, Analysed, or served up with a *Garnish;* besides, were Banks to take my case in hand, surely the others would follow, whereas if I had my first audience with lesser men, their fellows might still require *Persuasion.*

Having no other pressing Business, we headed out on foot the next morning, which we were relieved to see had dawned clear and crisp, the pestilent Fog having lifted, and autumnal breezes scoured the City of its effects. It was but a walk of perhaps ten minutes to Montagu House, which was home to the British Museum as well as the Royal Society; we ascended the front steps, and my Benefactor handed his Card to the uniformed doorman, mentioning that he had with him an introduction to Mr Banks.

'Very well, sir, you may go in — but your pig must remain outside,' added that gentleman, as we moved to enter.

'He's not *my* pig, sir — he is entirely his *own* — and it is he, specifically, that Mr Banks will most want to see,' Sam insisted.

'Is he then a *Specimen?*'

'Certainly not! I'll have you know Toby is an *Educated* pig; he has just completed a year of study at Oxford.'

This was too much for the doorman, who concluded that our visit must be some sort of Prank; he laid his hands on both of us, and forcibly escorted us down the stairs and out of the gate. I urged Sam to make the attempt alone, assuring him that I would not be in the least inconvenienced to Wait for him outside, but a glance from the doorman seemed to threaten even that attempt, and we backed off and slunk away down the street. Having failed in our first Foray into the lair of the Learned, we decided that we might fare better with Mr Sheldon. As Sam reminded me, Sheldon was prominent among those who had insisted that anatomy be pursued by the study of *Human* cadavers, whereas in the past surgeons had had to study Pigs in their place, and thus, despite his skill with the Knife, he was in fact a benefactor to my Kind. His Anatomical Museum in Tottenham-court Road was not much more than a mile distant, and we arrived there within the hour. The housekeeper who replied to our knock explained that the Museum was closed, but on Sam's mentioning our letter of introduction, asked us both in (though not without a bemused glance at my Person) and said she would deliver our message.

We found ourselves in a room walled with glass cases, within which stood a vast array of anatomical specimens, mostly skeletal and mounted, though there were some hanging from armatures, or floating within jars. Two or three complete human skeletons reclined — if that is the right word for it — in a corner, while in another recess were set row upon row of skulls. There was a distant sound of voices, then the determined series of steps that quickly brought to the doorway

the figure of Mr Sheldon. He was of modest height, with a sharp but not unfriendly
nose; he wore no wig, and his collar was
but loosely tied; over his coat he wore a sort
of muslin smock, and his sleeves bore the
stains of various powdery substances. He
looked at Sam, and then at me, and then at
Sam once more, seeming to suppress a
smile, but maintaining a serious and piercing gaze with his two grey eyes.

'Mr Samuel Nicholson?'

'Yes, sir.'

'And, let me see . . . *Toby,* is it?'

I made a slight and (I hoped) graceful
bow.

Mr Sheldon could hide his delight no
more, but broke into a wry smile. 'My good
fellows, word of your arrival precedes you
— I had a letter from Dr Adams a fortnight
ago — you are most welcome! But I must
confess, until I had seen you with my own
eyes, I was not certain of you — no, not
certain at all! But now that we have met, I
am sure we shall do each other great benefit!
Great benefit indeed!'

So saying, he motioned us to join him in a
small room adjoining, where some cheese
and bread had been set out for a modest
luncheon; at his summons, the maid
brought out two more loaves, and a bowl of

whey, which was set before me. He asked after our journey, and whether we had found our lodgings satisfactory, and laughed greatly at our account of our reception — or lack thereof — by the doorman at Montagu House.

'Well, Banks will see you — of that I have no doubt — but of course, he is frightfully busy, always is. The man's mind is like a copious index — an entry for every thing, but once entered, only consulted sporadically. Yes, that's it. But here, I think, we can do more for you, perhaps arrange for a little demonstration for some select friends. You would not be averse to that, Toby?'

'Not at all,' was my reply (Sam by this time having furnished me with my cards).

'Still, I must say, I was a little surprised to hear you are engaged upon the public stage as well. Can it be so?'

Sam and I looked at one another, our puzzlement quite evident.

'What — then is there no truth in the bills? Surely you have seen them.'

So saying, Mr Sheldon produced a handbill whose contents filled me with amazement (at first) and then with rage. The scoundrels! For here were my late fellows from my engagement at Astley's in Dublin — none other than Signore *Scaglioni,* Herr

Hautknochen, and 'La Belle Espagnole' —
and they were appearing with a creature
advertised as 'Toby, the Sagacious PIG, who
reckons the number of people present, tells
the time by a Gentleman's watch, and
distinguishes all sort of Colours' and all this
was to be seen, this very evening, at the
Theatre Royal at Sadler's Wells, for a mere
two shillings!

'This is a rank impostor!' I declared.

'Aha! I rather thought so. His talents did
seem a good deal more rudimentary than
yours,' he replied.

If I could have blushed, I would — my
consternation was evident.

'But what will you do? Surely your name
and reputation must be defended!'

'Maybe,' said Sam, 'we should attend the
show!'

'And what then?' Mr Sheldon shot back.
'A duel?'

'No, not a duel, but a Contest. Surely our
Toby here would carry away the laurels!'

'How do you propose to get him *in?*'

This was a more considerable problem.
For, however much people would flock to
behold an *Educated* Pig, there was (in my
experience) nary a Pig in attendance; nor
would one be expected. Any attempt I might
make to enter the premises would surely

raise unwanted attention, and cause such a stir that the hoped-for contest would be impossible.

'What if we were to issue a challenge?' asked Mr Sheldon. 'Invite this young Pretender, at a place and time of our choosing, and trounce him with your superior Knowledge and Skill! Surely he could not refuse.'

'That's it!' declared Sam. 'And we could have learned witnesses — yourself, sir, if you're willing — to vouch for the Results!'

To this Plan, I quickly gave my Assent, although not without some *Reservations.* For while I had little doubt that I would Prevail, I dreaded a return to my old life of the Shows, to which I had become quite Unaccustomed, and felt that, whoever the witnesses might be, there would be no preventing such a contest from becoming an untoward *Spectacle,* one at which even a Victory would not redound to my Benefit. Never the less, assured both by Sam and our new Friend that the circumstances would be most carefully Managed, and that every Care would be taken to ensure that our contest was purely *Intellectual* in nature, I decided to risk All. At its very base, there is nothing so like to burst that bubble *Reputation* as the Pin of a rival, a *poseur,* a *Dop-*

pelgänger who sits grinning in one's own Chair, and dares one to be seated!

Mr Sheldon took it in hand to write to the performers at Sadler's Wells, and had his letter delivered by messenger that same afternoon. We were pleased to receive a reply the next day, to the effect that our Challenge was accepted. As neutral ground, our opponents proposed the Academy Room at the Lyceum, Strand, where, just in the manner of a *Duel,* each side could propose its Weapons, and nominate its Seconds. A body of twelve men of good Reputation, six chosen by each Side, would serve as a sort of Jury, and Mr Lingham, the lessee of those Premises, would be the Chairman of this group *ex officio,* as a non-voting member, of course. Everything seemed to be in order, and we soon sat down to determine *Who,* among the many learned men we had at our disposal, would be ideal to serve upon our Panel.

With Mr Sheldon as our Ambassador, we quickly secured the services of Richard Kirwan and William Aiton; Sir Joseph Banks, alas, though he was not entirely unsympathetic to my *Plight,* sent his regrets, as he did not wish to appear a *Partisan* in any issue involving members of the Royal *Society.*

This left us still in need of *Three,* whom we sought through the Length and Breadth of Britain. Erasmus Darwin sent his regrets, explaining that his business in Birmingham required his attention throughout the period in question; James Keir, for similar reasons, could not afford to be absent from *Staffordshire.* Yet we were delighted to hear, a fortnight later, that William Cullen, the eminent physician, had at Dr Adams's urging agreed to be one of our Jury, as had Theophilus Lindsey, the theologian. For the final place, I held out the keenest Hope that Miss Seward would be willing to serve, and I even did her the Favour — which I have, I must say, to none other — of writing her a personal *Letter,* which I dictated to Sam. The text of this Letter is most deeply engraved in the Book of my Memory, and unfolded in this Fashion:

My dear Miss Seward,

It is with the utmost Respect that I write to you, who have on so many occasions proved to be a Friend, and yet whom I have never had the chance properly to Meet, or thank for your many Kindnesses. You will have heard, I do not doubt, that I am placed in fresh Difficulties here in

London, as both my name and reputation have been sullied by a Usurper, working in concert with a band of Ruffians — my late compatriots of the stage in Dublin. I have duly Challenged this Imitator, and he and I are to go to it at the Lyceum at the end of this present Month. There is to be empanelled a Jury, to judge the results of our Engagement, and each side may put forth six names. Were yours, my dear Miss Seward, to be enrolled upon on my list, I should count it one of the great honours of my so-far Brief existence, and it would bring me great Joy, regardless of the outcome of the Contest. You may reach me in care of Mr Sheldon, at the Royal Academy of Arts, 8 John Street, Strand.

I remain, as ever, your most Humble Servant,

Toby

After posting it, I lived in constant apprehension as to any *Reply,* such that I asked Mr Sheldon after it nearly every Morning, and several times begged him to call upon the Society's offices to check whether or not any word had been Received. I was, as a result, quite reduced to a quivering Bag of Nerves, which were again and again Jangled by the smallest inconvenience. You can imagine, then, my *Elation,* just over a week later, at receiving a reply in the Affirmative; indeed I have, ever since, carried this Letter close to my Bosom, by means of having it stitched into the lining of my Waistcoat:

My Dear Mr Toby,

Your appeal reached me this morning, and, not wishing to lose a Moment in reply, I will be brief. I should be delighted, and the Honour all mine, to have a place upon your Jury. You may count on my making an appearance, and I look forward very keenly to having at last the chance to Speak with you in Person (or should I say, in Pig?). I am more than confident as to the outcome of your upcoming Probation.

So take courage, my dear Toby!, and believe me always your friend and servant,
Anna Seward

14

By then, the appointed date for this contest of Pig versus *Pig* had drawn quite Near, and Sam and I had made the most thorough preparations: we had practised all our old Routines, gone over all our usual Signals, and even taken time to review my Latin grammar, of which I was justly proud — and certain that no porcine *poseur* could possibly match. We were also anxious to find out who had been chosen for the Jury by our opposition, but our requests for any account of this were Denied, with the word that we would know them when we saw them. Never the less, we were able, by following such fashionable gossip as anticipated the Event, to determine that there were, by all accounts, no men of Science or Learning among them. The best-known was Mr John Walter, a former coal-merchant who had taken up a career as a Publisher, and put out something called the *Daily Universal Register.* We were a little put off that such a man could both judge the contest and Write about it, but Mr Sheldon assured me that his Newspaper was a very small concern, and like to come to nothing, whereas he had already secured for us a promise to publish his own account in the London *Chronicle.*[1]

We arrived at the Premises early on the chosen Day that we might see the Arrangements of the place, and adapt ourselves to them. Ordinarily employed as a sort of lecture hall, the Lyceum had been modified slightly for this event, with a low platform erected at its Front for our *Performances,* and two rows of six chairs placed along the right-hand side of the hall, which comprised the *Jury's* 'box'. We were very nearly the first to arrive, and were greeted with great Warmth by Mr *Lingham,* a portly gentleman of perhaps sixty years of age. He seemed to take great delight in his rooms becoming

1. This, I should like to add, was the one piece of bad advice I ever Receiv'd from Mr Sheldon, as this 'small concern' was later to be known as *The Times* of London, and be the principal organ of the Metropolis.

the scene of such an *Affair* for (as he showed us in a book of press clippings he kept) the matter of the 'Learned Pig' was very much the Talk of the Town. I was somewhat astonished to Read for the first time what some *Wags* had to say on the Matter: no less a light than *Sheridan* proclaimed me 'a far greater object of admiration to the English nation than ever was Sir Isaac *Newton*' while an anonymous Bard epitomiz'd me thus in *Verse:*

> A *gentle* pig this Toby is, a real pig of
>   Parts,
> As learnéd as an F.R.S. or graduate in
>   Arts;
> His ancestors, 'tis true, alas, could only
>   grunt and squeak,
> But He has been at *Oxford* — and in a
>   week shall *Speak.*

I had to admit, I basked in the glow of these Lines for more than a moment, although it was not quite Accurate to say that I should merely *Speak,* when in fact what I did was to *Spell,* a talent which the greater part of the 'English Nation' at that time, jabber as they might, did not possess.

As we peered over these *Documents,* a number of other parties arrived, including

Mr Walter and several other Men whom we took to be his co-jurors. None was known to us, but Mr Lingham was kind enough to give us their names: they were Joseph Sparkes, of the East India Company, Thomas Farr, a Liverpool merchant, James Sanderson, an Alderman, and Henry Blundell, of the Africa Company. All these men were similarly dressed, similarly deported and similarly *Wigged;* indeed, I could hardly recall a Farrow of new *Pigs* that looked more alike. For their part, I am sure none of them had made the acquaintance of any Animal, save as a piece of Merchandise, nor had any Notion of any Sapient beings unlike themselves; they may as well have been Visitors from some other celestial Sphere, as any more familiar Creatures. The last of their Number shortly arrived, whom we recognised at once, for here was Charles *Dibdin,* the illustrious Actor — but his presence did not at all cheer us, for we feared that, as a business associate of Mr Astley, he was very likely to vote in favour of the *Pretender.*

Our own jurors had also begun to arrive, and each of them stopt to pay their brief Respects; as might be expected from men whose life was of the Mind, they made a far more Rumpled and irregular *Set* than their

Mercantile colleagues. Richard Kirwan was the most Dignified of the Bunch, his head held aloft with the aid of a tight swathe of neckerchiefs; William Aiton, the botanist, was far more *Loosely* attired in a blue frock and grey waistcoat, wearing a red wig that matched his ruddy countenance. William Cullen then billowed in upon the Sails of his black academic Gown, his face radiating both Kindness and Acuity, and with him Theophilus Lindsey who, though more reserved, bore the Expression of a man whose Sobriety seemed always about to burst forth into a *Grin.* Of course I was most anxious, and not a little *Shy,* of meeting Miss Seward, and was enormously relieved when she appeared at last. From the moment she entered the room, it seemed to me as though the world contained but Herself and me, and all the rest were merely a species of Bystander. She wore an enormous dress of violet *Taffeta,* secured about her waist with a cincture of dark velvet; her Hair, which one could see was all her *Own,* was tied back with a ribbon of like material, and her face quite Glowed with the vivacity of a Woman who knows her own *Purposes,* and likely those of others as well.

She curtsied lightly before me, and I Bowed as best I could, and by means of

Sam and our small cards, we were at least able to make our *Introductions.*

'Mr Toby, it is an honour finally to Meet you.'

'Madam, the honour is all mine. I am most glad to see you!'

'And I you! Have no fear — why, I believe that those Periwigs over there have not the *Least* idea of your true abilities — but you will show them, of that I am certain.'

'Your confidence is most Heartening — I shall do my very best to Repay it.'

And then it was time to take the *Stage.* Curiously, although I had been told he was present, my Rival was not yet in evidence; the explanation of this came when, through a sidedoor cleverly concealed as a section of the Wall, he and his *Man* entered. It was a strange and Uncanny thing to behold another creature as curiously Removed from Nature as myself, and yet what first struck my Eye were our enormous differences. If I was large and Pink, he was small and *Black,* with a fine bristle of hair that looked to have been lately *combed.* It was not an uncomely appearance, and while he, too, had a fancy Waistcoat, his was of a rich *Crimson,* which nicely complemented his dusky complexion. I could not, alas, say as much for his Master, whose lumpy, corpulent form was ill-squeezed into a ridiculous green Frock coat, his plump head plopped above his Lace neckerchief like a Tomato upon a *Napkin.* Never the less, despite his unpleasant appearance, he bowed courteously and low (as did my *Sam*), and conducted himself with dignity throughout the Proceedings.

We were first given a series of *Questions* submitted by the Jury, most of them very rudimentary ones that admitted of a brief answer: what was the capital of France, what country lay to the West of England, how many gills in a Pint, and so forth. Both my rival and I managed all of them without fault, although at one point I came close to accidentally dropping one of my Letters, as I stumbled upon an irregular Board in the platform. On and on it went, until it became quite clear that such questions would settle no Matter but that of sheer *Endurance.* We were next given questions that had been written out in block letters upon cards, which I found my counterpart could Read as well as I, though whether through his own Sense or prior training I could not tell. Next, we were asked to tell the Time displayed upon a Pocket watch, another task we both managed with alacrity. Clearly, these were all as much a part of the other

Pig's *repertoire* as they were of mine, and none was likely to disclose a shade of Difference between us.

As arranged, our next round was conducted in Latin, and involved the declension of nouns of various kinds, along with the conjugation of Verbs. I had expected them to have prepared for the test, but was amazed to see how quickly my Competitor laid out his A-M-O, A-M-A-S, and A-M-A-T; he fairly leapt to his letters, and although I did my best, I could barely manage to keep pace with him, and was quite soon Out of *Breath*. Simple sentences were then demanded of us, with the words spoken out loud leaving us the task of spelling them, and again neither my dark *Opponent* nor myself made any missteps. And so the sentences continued one after another, droning along in my Brain like the repeated march of a pair of Boots over the same piece of *Ground*. Finally, when I felt I could stand it no more, I ran across the stage, knocking over my opponent's table where his cards stood at the ready, and quickly spelt out from the resulting heap of letters this question: Q-U-O U-S-Q-U-E T-A-N-D-E-M — which is to say, How much longer?

There was a stunned Silence among all present; then a murmur of puzzlement swept through Jury and Spectators alike. Mr *Lingham,* taking his role as Judge to heart, pounded with his Gavel upon the railing, calling for 'order in the court', but the sight was so unintentionally Comic, that it only Added to the chaos. At last Dr Cullen, who had earlier been elected Foreman by his fellow *Jurors,* stood and called for silence.

'Gentlemen! Gentlemen! Please! I ask you to recall the Dignity of this occasion; we are here to exercise our Rational faculties, not our Passions!'

This was followed by general grunts of agreement, and expectant silence.

'I would call your attention to the following points: one, that for more than an hour, we have given our two Subjects every kind of Test that their abilities — or so we supposed — permitted, and Both have acquitted themselves without Error. Two, that there are two Measures of good Learning — the fair Reply, and the intelligent Question, and that the Latter is by far the greater. Three, that *Toby* here, who is by all accounts at least the Elder of our contestants, finding himself in a state of Exasperation, has shown himself capable of this second and more Profound evidence of Understanding. For anything that can be done by Rules, whether it is telling the Time or declining Nouns, can be learnt by *Rote*, but the spontaneous generation of Discourse, though it follows these, cannot be *made* by them; it is, as the poet Dante once re-marked, written deep within the spirit and is there formed *sine omnia regula* — without any rules.'

Here he cleared his throat, and I thought I saw him suppress a little smile.

'We of the Jury have accordingly discussed this matter among ourselves, and it is our unanimous View that *Toby* — that is, he of long association with Mr Silas Bisset and Mr Samuel Nicholson — has earned the *Laurels* in this affair. This court is now concluded, and young Toby's question has its answer.'

And there was great rejoicing. I was con-gratulated by all present, and showered with encomiums too numerous and generous to mention without embarrassment. Yet at that same moment, watching my late Opponent and his man picking up their scattered cards, I felt a terrible sense of Shame, not simply for what I had done, but for ever having Agreed to such a humiliating contest. For not the first time, I reflected that it was quite as Degrading to be poked and prodded by the scrutinising fingers of Science as to be gawped at and jeered by the most unwashed of the human *Masses.* I wished for nothing more than to share these sentiments with my counterpart, but I could see already in his eyes the twin flickers of fear that revealed at once to me the *Brutality* of his Master. I endeavoured to Intervene, but before I could attract the attention of any of my Friends, both Pig and Man had disappeared through the same concealed door through which they had entered. I resolved, come what may, that I would find some means of liberating my darker cousin from his unjustified Confinement.

It was to Miss Seward I turned in this resolve, and although I had to wait until the furore died down, she proved very Receptive to my plea. We had, by that time, retired to Mr Sheldon's rooms, where the members of the party of the 'victorious Pig' were saluting each other with glasses of Tokay. I declined to join in the revelry — I have never in my life imbibed any spirituous liquors, having throughout my career had far too many occasions to witness the behaviour of Humans once in their grasp — but never the less was very much relieved that at last these Proceedings were over. A few of the members of the Jury joined us, although to my regret Dr Cullen had to depart early, as he was very anxious to return to the company of his students at Edinburgh. Mr Aiton proved to be the liveliest of the group, proposing all manner of Toasts, and offering it as his opinion that I was the most remarkable *Oddity* of Nature ever known. I took some umbrage at this term, which Sam and Mr Sheldon instantly perceived, and the latter offered in rejoinder that the practice of Language was as Odd in one being as another, since no creature was to its usage born, and human children themselves had to Acquire it by practice.

He recalled an experiment variously attributed to Frederick II or Constantine the Great, in which the learned monarch wished to determine which Language was most original to man. To satisfy his curiosity in this matter, a small boy of scarcely three months age was confined within a chamber deep within the Palace, and provided with a deaf-mute as a wet nurse. The absolute Rule was that no one should speak a word of any language within hearing of the poor lad, although he was fed and cared for decently enough; once he had reached the age of twelve years, he was brought before the King, and made to understand by signs that he should speak. The unfortunate youth then showered the present company with horrid speech, all of a guttural and noisome quality, out of which the wise men present could make out only 'El el el el el' — on the basis of which they declared that the word was in fact 'El' — that is לא, which signifies 'God' — and that thus Hebrew was the original language of humankind. All present laughed at the absurdity of such a procedure, save myself: I thought only of the child's long years of confinement, and the unlikelihood of his discovering any happiness in life, having been so long deprived.

It was after the recounting of this Anecdote, and once the conversation had returned to a more uniform Buzz, that I took Sam aside with me and approached Miss Seward. I explained, as briefly and forcefully as I could, how convinced I was that my late opponent was under the Thumb of a Brute, and must now be in fear for his *Life,* for having lost the contest in which we had been so publicly Engaged. She at once perceived the gravity of the situation, and summoned Mr Lindsey to our colloquy. That reverend gentleman at once suggested we send for a young acquaintance of his, a Mr Wilberforce, who was already at the age of twenty-five a Member of Parliament, and who had begun to take the strongest interest in the Anti-Slavery cause. Surely such a man would recognise as readily the inhumanity of man to Animal evident in my unhappy Comrade's situation, and surely a man of his energy and convictions would take action to see him *Freed.*

Mr Lindsey made the arrangements, and that very evening we called upon Mr Wilberforce in his chambers. I was, perhaps, even more anxious at this moment than when I had first trod upon the greens at Oxford, for if the lawns of learning were unaccustomed to porcine prints, the steps of Parliament seemed even *more* so. I recalled with bitterness having been turned away at the British *Museum,* and called a 'specimen' — what would be the result here at the hands of these bewigged and booted guards? Happily, Mr Wilberforce spared me any embarrassment by coming down himself, and welcoming us within, in such a graceful and natural manner that the guards simply remained at attention — for if a Member wished to welcome a Pig, who were they to question him? His easy manner and warmth of speech made one instantly at ease, and more than any Human I have ever encountered, Mr Wilberforce treated me just as he would any of his two-legged constituents, without the slightest hint of condescension.

Once we had been seated, he enquired of me at once about the nature of our visit, and watched attentively as I spelt out my concerns. I had been witness, I declared, to far more than my measure of cruelty, both of human to *Human,* and human to *Animal.* Indeed, it was my sorrow to observe that Homo 'Sapiens' was by far the cruellest of all creatures, for no other Animal I had ever known took such pleasure in the wanton injury of another. Wolves devoured their prey, and cats pounced upon mice, with infinitely more mercy than malicious Man, whose crime was made worse by the endless *Justifications* of his Brutality with which he cloaked his conscience. Mr Wilberforce was so taken by my account that, or so it seemed to me, he was almost moved to tears, and several times grew flushed in the face. Last of all, I recounted my contest with the Pig I admitted I had once demeaned as a mere *Pretender,* and explained how, by long experience of seeing the same, I could read the flicker of fear in his eyes as readily as any Bill of Indictment: here was a victim of cruelty, cruelty inflicted for the purpose of another's Profit.

As soon as I had finished, Mr Wilberforce took up his hat and coat, and summoned a carriage. We had earlier obtained from Mr Lingham the address at which my rival and his keeper were supposed to have lodged, and we at once sped thither, regardless of the weather, which had grown cold and blustery as the day went on, and was now breaking into storm. A few moments brought us to the place, a grimy Inn in the vicinity of Limehouse *Hole*. A few drunken barge-men lay senseless in the street outside, and there was a general sound of clamour within, but as we had brought with us two of the Yeomen of Westminster, we hesitated not at all to step inside. The owner of the Inn, though at first a bull of Bluster, was reduced to a quavering heap of *jelly* as soon as our guards confronted him with their Pikestaffs, and we mounted the stairs without opposition. We came soon to the room in which dwelt the Man whose cruelty I already knew without seeing — *and woe is me, to see what I have seen!*

The room was strewn with filthy straw; its sole features were a rough-hewn table, at which our Man was seated, bibbed and squatting before a greasy trencher, and a rusty Cage, within which my fellow creature was confined, with scarce an inch in any direction where he could move his Limbs. That this cage had never been Cleaned was attested at once by the evidence of our *Nostrils;* the horrid admixture of man's food and animal feculence would have brought a lesser soul to his knees. Mr Wilberforce, however, was sustained by the fierce air of his indignation, and at once ordered his officers to take the Man into their custody. This act was not taken kindly.

'I say! Sir! What are you doing? Here I am, a poor man about to take his meal, and you accost me by force? What do you mean by this?'

'I say to you, Sir, what are *you* doing? Dare you to take your repast, while this poor Creature lies confined within a space in which he is scarce able to Breathe? I am tempted to say, Sir, that it is you who are the Pig in this room — but I refrain from doing so, for such would be an Insult to a Species which, in fact, is far more *Human* than you!'

'What right have you to seize me thus? What have these palace Guards to do with a place like this? On whose authority am I grappled?'

'Whose authority? You may take your choice, sir: on the authority of *God* upon whose Commandments you have trampled; on the authority of this Nation, whose character you have stained; or on my personal authority as a sworn member of this present Parliament of Great Britain and Ireland. I arrest you in all their names, and you may lodge your Appeal with whomever you please!'

After the Man, whose name, or so we were informed, was Mr John *Fawkes,* had been led away, we turned our attentions to his unfortunate *Pig.* Deprived of his crimson waistcoat, and the other trappings of his Act, he presented a very piteous Sight; his hair was uncombed, his backside showed welts from the lashes of a bamboo Cane (which instrument stood near at hand against the wall), and his two hind legs were afflicted with sores where they had rubbed against the bars of his Cage. We at once conveyed him to our carriage, using a board and a bedsheet as a sort of improvised Pallet, and thence to Mr Sheldon's. That kind and capable gentleman then ministered to my unfortunate cousin with all the care he would have lavished upon any Human patient; he was set up in a spacious enclosure, provided with fresh straw, and nursed back to Health with infinite patience. Within a week, the sores were nearly healed, and he was able to move about without discomfort, and a few days later we thought it proper to bring him his Cards, that he and I might enjoy a porcine *Parley,* something which — so far as I know — had never been attempted before, or Since.

He was hesitant at first to take up his *Letters,* and I could well imagine why: having only fetched them before under the threat of the Lash, it was something new and strange for him to select them on his own, without the nervous glance over his shoulder that had become so habitual to his being. At last, though, he overcame his trepidation, and told me something of his History, which greatly *Amazed* me. He had been born in Dublin, and it was — or so he was later told — on account of my appearance at *Astley's* that his proprietor had been inspired to acquire him. This man's real name was not Fawkes but *Schmidt;* he had been given the nickname 'Fawkes' as a youth, on account of his fierce temper and tendency to *Explode,* which it was no surprise to learn. On the departure of Mr Bisset and myself, he went to the Dublin market and made for a stall of suckling *Pigs,* from which he selected the one he thought the most apt to Training — which was, of course, my unlucky Comrade.

Mr Schmidt then brought him to his residence, which was in the poorer quarter of the City, and kept him in a tiny and squalid *Yard,* a sort of accidental gap between the tenements, which deeply shadowed it on every side and was used by the inhabitants to toss refuse and the contents of their chamberpots. From this unhappy abode he was brought, three times a day, to a small room Mr Schmidt had rented for the purpose, where he was given his training. At first, he had only to jump upon a box and through a Hoop; after that he was given his first few letters, and asked to choose the one demanded; any mistake resulted in an instantaneous blow with the bamboo. He quickly learnt them all, but his Education then reached an *Impasse,* as Mr Schmidt was unable himself to Spell or write anything more than his Name. A second, kinder, man was brought in; but despite their long acquaintance, he never learnt this man's name, calling him simply 'the Gentleman'. This man trained him in spelling, reproving his mistakes with only a glance, and rewarding his better efforts with a piece of a turnip or a handful of sweet oats. As his ordinary fare was the worst sort of swill, he laboured greatly to please this Gentleman, and within the next few months, was as capable a Speller as any schoolboy.

Once these lessons were complete, alas, my friend never saw the man again. Mr Schmidt enquired at *Astley's,* and was told they had no further place for such an Act — but from them he learnt the names of the acrobats with whom I had shared the bill, and tracked them down to Manchester, where they were then appearing. Sceptical at first, they eventually added him to their programme on two nights of the week, and the interest of the Audience — stirred up, I do not doubt, by my own appearances in the same part of the Country — grew substantially. There was nothing so self-evidently *Profitable* as to name this pig 'Toby' as well, for in that way the Public was readily led to believe him the very same animal, and indeed every particle of his *Act* was modelled upon mine. In a few cases, such as the mind-reading trick, the system evaded the (rather limited) capacity of Mr Schmidt's *understanding,* and so it was simply left off the bills. By sundry turns, as the acrobatic troupe wound its way towards London for the autumn season, this act became their star attraction, but this proved to be of little benefit to my *alter Ego.* For, just as his master gained in wealth and reputation, so he increased in *Cruelty,* even though there was no longer any Call for it, other than to satisfy his degraded sense of Enjoyment, in the wilful infliction of Pain upon another.

The last few weeks had been the worst of his life, he told me: he had had to learn Latin, as his master knew it was sure to be part of our Contest. For this purpose, Mr Schmidt had brought in another man, no gentleman in his conduct but apparently a Graduate of one of the Universities, and he was just as cruel and sharp as his master, if not more so. To be beaten for improperly conjugating the verbs that signified Love, and Help, and Hope — *spero, speras, sperat, speramus!* — was a terrible thing indeed. When the contest was lost, he was certain he was to be beaten viciously, or even sold to a slaughterhouse, as his master often threatened when he was in his *Cups*, but our arrival on the very evening of his defeat had saved him from either fate, for which he was eternally Grateful.

And then this other Toby made a singular request — one that surprised me at the time, but which I now regard as a sure sign of his native *Wisdom*. He asked to have his Cards burnt, and never to have to spell again. He knew that, were this done, he would never again be able to communicate with me or with any one, and while he regretted the loss, he considered that his life, looked at in full, would be a far richer and happier one if he never again felt the taste of pasteboard in his mouth, or had to squint against the stage-lights amidst a jeering crowd as he trotted back and forth. I endeavoured to persuade him to postpone so Rash and irrevocable a plan, to wait a while, and then to take a place alongside me, as my companion and my Cohort, and enjoy the kindest treatment, never having to take the Stage again, if that were his wish. But he refused all my entreaties, both with kindness and with firmness, and so we at last consented to his Desire. The very next day, we burnt his cards in the side-yard of Mr Sheldon's museum, retaining only one — *P* — as a sort of souvenir. Mr Wilberforce, who as ever maintained the keenest interest in the future of his porcine Ward, had provided him a permanent place at his farm at Marden Park in Surrey, where he would be for ever free from any demands, and kept in safety and comfort until the end of his days, whenever that might be. Scarcely a week later, he was conveyed there by a hired coach; along with the rest of his London friends, I saw him off that chilly morning. We lined up along the edge of the Tottenham-court Road, the men with their

212

hats in their hands, and I received his final Token: the crimson waistcoat he had worn upon the stage. In the end, neither our letters nor all our *Words* would have been of any comfort or use: we simply bade each other good-bye with our *Eyes*.

15

The abrupt retirement of my esteemed Comrade to his country residence left a deep and persistent feeling of melancholy in its wake. The mood was further darkened by the news, which came only a few days later, of the death of Dr Adams, who had been such an excellent friend and patron of the Arts; in his absence, I knew, it would be impossible for me to return to my studies at Oxford. I found myself at a strange *Impasse,* with disenchantment at every Door: I had little wish to return to the Stage, for the words of my erstwhile rival had only strengthened my *Conviction* that such a Life was unsuited to any Animal with a sense of pride or dignity; but with the path to Learning now foreclosed, I knew not where next to turn. Sam and I were quite content with each other's Company, and Mr Sheldon was most anxious that we remain, and placed his private Library at our disposal as an enticement. This, for a time, was contentment enough, as I was able at last to read according to my Pleasure, and spent many a profitable afternoon perusing the works of the Poets, among whom *Shakespeare* became a special favourite. Never the less, despite these rich and convenient pleasures, I was restless; having come of age upon the Road, I was ill at ease with a Sedentary life, however well provided. There remained so much I had not seen, and I longed to travel to distant Lands, and take in the wonders of the habitable World.

But, as so often it chanced to happen in my singular career, I was soon obliged to set aside these plans, and acquiesce to the demands of the *Fashionable* world. Having taken a subscription to the London *Chronicle,* I of course regularly browsed the columns in which Amusements were advertised, and was quite taken aback one day to discover that, once again, I had a Rival upon the Stage — indeed, as it turned out, not just one but *Two.* The rage for educated Pigs — and horses, dogs, and even *Fish* — seemed unquenchable, and into the Void my absence from the public Eye had left, stept many an upstart, and many a brutish

Imitator. The first of these at first caused me great distress, as it seemed to me that here was another poor, exploited creature — the notice spoke of the Pig's *instant* compliance with its Master's commands — and so of course I at once sent word to Mr Wilberforce, and together we went to Mr Hughes's Royal *Circus,* the rival of Mr Astley's establishment, with a demand to see his new Act, and satisfy ourselves that the Animal concerned was being treated humanely.

Mr Hughes, a sharp-faced man with the practised step and voice of a veteran showman, welcomed us into his office. As soon as he had heard our case, he burst out laughing uproariously, so much so that he could scarce contain himself, despite Mr Wilberforce's evident and growing anger. At last he held up his hands, resumed his serious demeanour, and bade us follow him into a room behind the stage of the Circus, where the sundry stools, ladders, steps and other props of the show were kept. He led us around to a large pedestal of polished wood, upon which was a figure draped with a linen sheet. Bowing, just as he would to open a new act, he at once drew back the cloth, to our utter and absolute amazement.

'Gentlemen, behold! Here is the learned Pig you seek! And yet, I am afraid, you may find him a little *unresponsive,* as he's badly in want of winding!'

There upon the plinth we saw a *Pig* indeed — a Pig of brass and silvered sheen, with hoofs of ebon and a nose of polished *Copper,* his eyes a pair of carbuncles and a tail of twisted Iron. Up along one of the rear legs of the figure, we could see a number of wires and cogs, through which we surmised the actions of the figure were controlled. We had to laugh ourselves, then, to see how we had been deceived — we had come to help a fellow creature, and had encountered only a clever *Facsimile,* a mere mechanical *manqué* whose 'well-being' would better be attended to with an oil-can and a polishing-cloth than with Oats or Straw. Mr Hughes then briefly explained the act, in which the pig would seem to eat, and then excrete, its food, would stamp its forelegs for simple sums of Arithmetic, and then answer questions from the audience, shaking its head up and down for 'Yes' and from side to side for 'No'. It seemed to me a rather limited set of possibilities, but Mr Hughes assured us that, in the hands of the pig's inventor and proprietor — the eminent mechanic-showman Signor *Spinetti* — it provided ample material for a fifteen-minute pantomime, which formed the *Entr'acte* between thc bareback riders and the rope-dancers.

My second encounter with a swinish Simulacrum came scarcely a fortnight later, in the form of a handbill pasted upon the hoardings adjacent to the King's Concert Rooms, not far from Mr Sheldon's museum. 'THE WONDERFUL PIG OF KNOWLEDGE,' declared the bill, 'UNDER THE DIRECTION OF SIEUR *GARMAN,* lately arrived from *PARIS,* where he appeared with enormous Success for more than twenty weeks with his "COCHON SAVANT" at the Amphitheatre *Anglois.*' The main feature of the bill was a large woodcut depicting a pig picking out a letter from a heap under the direction of a man in a riding outfit holding a Stick, above which dangled a ribbon on which was inscribed 'LE MIEUX COCHON SAVANT DU SIEUR GARMAN', which, though I had but little acquaintance with French, was clear enough — a boast at *My* expense!

Here I must in frankness admit that it was not Charity but *Envy* I felt upon seeing this boastful claim, and the more so as the pig's particulars — counting the number of Persons in attendance, telling the time, even reading the minds of Ladies — were all abstracted from my own Act. That a *French-man* should make such claims also pricked my pride, for although I would hardly have said that I had any especially warm feelings for my Native land, I never the less felt that such claims impinged upon the originality and capability of *Britain* as much as on my own. And so at first I hurried to speak with Sam, desiring that he assist me in finding some way to Spy out this new Rival, but as before there seemed no way for me to attend such a show without drawing Notice. I had little appetite for another *Contest,* doubted indeed that the Public would — and yet, try as I might, I could not rid myself of the feeling that I must somehow answer this Injustice, and reclaim my preeminence in the Pantheon of Pigs, such as it was. There seemed nothing for it but a return to the Stage, although both Sam and I were most Reluctant to revive our past productions.

At just that moment, happily, we received a Letter from Dr Cullen, in which that excellent gentleman invited us to pay him a visit in *Edinburgh,* as he was anxious to acquaint us with Friends of his there, and perhaps offer some demonstration of my Skill to the sceptical among his *Colleagues.* Sam and I at once considered that, were we to accept this invitation, we could work our way Northwards by degrees, proclaiming this our *Farewell* tour, and concluding in Edinburgh. Under the consideration that this would be my final set of Appearances, I was delighted to consent; we could now Answer the Challenge, and offer the World a last opportunity to see the *Original* Sapient Pig. Of course, there could be little doubt that there would be Rivals and Successors yet to come, but once we were embarked upon the road, they could little trouble us there. 'He who is tired of London, is tired of *Life,*' Dr Johnson used to say — but it seemed to me then that the sooner I could quit that City, the sooner I would be rid (at least) of the more proximate and Numerous of my competitors, and able to find a way through the world that would truly be my *Own.*

As a favour to Mr Lingham, we agreed to open our Tour in the Academy Room at the Lyceum, and there, over the three weeks that followed, we enjoyed an unbroken run of full houses. Whether it was because the Public accepted my claim that I was, after all, the only true Original Pig of my kind, or because we had repapered every wall and *Hoarding* in London with our Handbills, or because of the quality of our Act, I could not say, but it was immensely gratifying no matter what its Cause. For this tour, we made a quite deliberate decision to leave behind all our other *Animal* players; Mr Lockyer had attended to them throughout our stay in the City and had so grown in affection for them that he was loath to part with their company, and so those among our Cats, our Monkeys, Dogs, Birds and the Hare that yet lived were suffered to remain with him. We planned only to take our Horses, and rebuilt our Wagon along the lines of a Gypsy's Caravan, with a capacious interior room divided into accommodations for Sam and myself. Our itinerary was designed to include as many of our previous Venues as possible, including a stop at Oxford to visit my old College, and a visit to the place of my Birth in Salford (where still, for all that we knew, Sam's uncle yet kept his farm), and Chester, going from thence up the coast to Glasgow, and concluding in Edinburgh.

Our Act comprised all of the best features of all we had done before, including reading and writing, a session of Latin verbs, and the ever-popular 'reading' of the minds of ladies in attendance — this time with the written assurance on our bills that 'Toby never divulges the thoughts of any Lady in the company *but by her permission.*' Two innovations were made: the First a game of *Whist,* which was easy for me, as I had played it quite regularly with Sam and others over the years; the Second a tableau, which we dubbed 'Animal Magnetism' after the notions of Franz *Mesmer,* whose ideas were much discussed at the court of Louis XVI and elsewhere — Monsieur *Garman* had such an act, and we thought we could readily do him one Better. Our version consisted of a pantomime of porcine Distress, in which I seemed to Eat something that caused me great pain, at which Sam would play the Doctor and attend to me by passing a series of magnets over my prostrate form; this effected a Miraculous cure, and ended with doctor and Patient cavorting about the Stage to the accompaniment of a *Fiddle.*

The notices were full of the highest praise, but our real satisfaction came when we had word that Monsieur Garman had announced, with the showman's usual flair of turning poor returns into good news, that 'the incessant demands of the Irish public' had obliged him to end his show early and embark for Dublin. This news came on the afternoon of our final London show, and I will not exaggerate if I tell you that it lent considerable extra Verve to that evening's performance, turning Pacing to Prancing, Bows into Genuflections, and mere Spelling into the most elegant *Orthography*. We did three curtain calls and an Encore, and retired to a reception at Mr Lindsey's rooms, which lay only a short walk away. All our London friends were there; Miss Seward had been so kind as to return for a final Visit, as had Mr Kirwan and Mr Aiton; among the many others who honoured us with their presence were Mr Wilberforce, Sir Joseph Banks, the painter Mr Benjamin *West* and his wife, and another neighbour, John Flaxman, a sculptor of some repute. Mr Flaxman introduced to me a young Engraver by the name of Mr Blake, and pressed upon me a volume of the young man's poetry, which had lately been imprinted by Mr Flaxman's *Aunt*. This little book I gladly accepted, and in later years I have often reflected on its being the first in the career of a truly astonishing *Poet*.

At last, we had to say our final 'adoos' and retire to make the most of what remained of the night, for we were pledged to commence upon our Tour the next morning. We stayed, of course, at Mr Sheldon's, and I should like to note here that gentleman's enormous and unfailing Kindness to us in every regard, which was essential to our London success, as well as our future fortunes. It was with a genuine feeling of *Distress* that we parted the next morning, which I would not do until I extracted from him a promise to visit us in Edinburgh at his earliest possible convenience. Our horses and wagon having been brought round the night before, and every thing placed in readiness, we set out at last upon the road to Oxford by way of Uxbridge. And, although the buildings, the streets and the dreary tide of humanity were much the same, I could not help but reflect on how much had changed since my arrival in London only a few short months before. I had tasted *Fame* — of a rare sort — but had also seen ignominy, and found that men of *Science,* ultimately, have the same tastes and desires as other men; their natures were, it seemed to me, as divided as my *Own.*

For what was I? A freak of nature? But if I were, might not Sir Isaac Newton, or Galileo, or *Shakespeare* be similarly regarded as freaks? One model of existence — the more popular, I should say — imagines the young as empty vessels, ready to be filled with the Stuff of *Learning,* and entirely creatures of such training; your average human *scholler* was in this case no more, and no less, a product of his schooling than I. But if, instead, there lay within *some,* but not all, souls a certain indefinable Spark of genius, which required only sufficient *Tinder* to set the world ablaze, then all such men were Freaks, and there was no more point in trying to produce such fellows through mere Learning than there was in lecturing to *Stones* to make them capable. It seemed that Nature, alas, far from being the hand-maiden of Genius, was in fact far better adapted to cultivate enormous herds of *Mediocrity,* whether of human or Porcine race, than she was to nurture Singularities.

It was with these thoughts in my Mind that I watched the great Metropolis of London dwindle into its Suburbs, and fade into its country Environs; the sight seemed to me no more, and no less, than the diminishment into distance of an enormous *Sty.*

16

Of our exhibitions in the course of our northward Progress, I will say *little,* for there is — in truth — very little worth saying. It was, of course, gratifying to find that my Reputation had not been in any way Diminished, either by the passage of Time or by Rival Pigs, for our shows were well attended in every Town, and in all sorts of Weather. In Oxford, I was gratified to meet with some of my former fellows at Pembroke, as was Sam; we were, however, disheartened to discover that Dr Adams had been buried in Gloucester, which we could not reach given our existing commitments for our *Tour.* We contented ourselves by making a small donation in his name to the College, as well as to a fund that was being taken up to place a Memorial in Gloucester *Cathedral.* From there we retraced the steps of our former passage, revisiting our old venues at Banbury, Coventry, Stafford and *Crewe.* We at last drew near to the valley of the river *Irwell,* in the vicinity of *Salford,* not far from the place of my Birth. On our previous Tours, I had always taken care to avoid the area, being none too sure as to my Reception there. But now, on this my final tour of Britain, it seemed only just to call upon the place of my *Origin,* if only to reflect on the enormous distance I had travelled, both physically and spiritually, since my being there.

We took the precaution of having with us in our company a Mr John *Tipping,* one of the Constables of the city of *Manchester.* He was a jovial fellow, who recalled having seen our show some years previous in Liverpool, and was only too happy to Protect us, should we encounter any threats of *violence* against Pig or *Person.* And yet, though he accompanied us as a Friend, I could not help but think on that other Constable, who gave Mr Bisset such a thrashing that I fear he never truly recovered; indeed I believe it was a principal cause of his *Death.* As we came down the old lane that led to Lloyd Farm, I felt a strange sensation indeed, as though the entire Narrative of my Life were running crazily Backward, like a Moving

Panorama gone off its Spools. Here, indifferent save by a few fence-posts that were perhaps more Askew than before, or a Hedgerow that had grown in size and wildness, was the very road I had first taken when Mr Lloyd brought me to *Market* — ah, how that word now Resonated within me. For, having once gone off to be Marketed, I wondered whether such Vending had ever really Ceased, or simply changed its venue and its Rates. What do I hear for the Learned Pig?

But when we came to the Farm itself, I could see at a glance, as could we all, that we had come too *Late*. The Gate was in a sad state, its leather latch long gone, and the whitewash rained away from stone and lath. The gravel path that once led to the front door was almost entirely obscured by Weeds, and the House itself — such as we could make it out — was practically overtaken by Vegetation, as though the Earth would swallow it entire. There could be no doubt that no active Hand had overseen the farm for some time, and that Mr Lloyd — were he still extant — must long ago have left the premises. We poked about, idly, and I spied the rotted ruin of the Shed that had once adjoined my Sty, but of the place itself we could only guess its outlines by the undulations of the soil, and the rankness of the vegetation that grew taller and darker where once our Swill had been poured out to us, and where my *Mother* — of whom I could scarce recall more than a shadow's shadow — had dwelt. *Tempus fugit, non autem memoria!*

We did not linger at the spot, but pressed onwards with our *Tour,* for the Season was growing late, and our road yet stretched out long before us. Our next stop was Lancaster, which we reached by way of the villages of Walkden, Chorley and Scorton, passing through many a stretch of open country, and many a desolate mere. As we came into the outskirts of the town, we could see upon the horizon the looming form of Lancaster Castle, an imposing edifice that from time immemorial had housed one of the principal of His Majesty's *Prisons,* and a notorious one as well; here it was that the Preston Witches had been hanged nearly two centuries past, and the gallows still stood from which they had dangled. We dared not approach the castle that evening, preferring to lodge at the White Cross Inn, which stood at the city's edge near the ancient foundation of the Knights Hospitallers, which gave the district its Name.

Our performance here was to be at a new *Theatre*, which had been established in St Leonard's Street, in the northeastern corner of the city. The proprietor, a Mr Charles *Whitlock*, anxious to gain for the place the reputation of a legitimate House, had been hesitant to make any Engagement with us; it was only (so we were told) after Mr *Dibdin* wrote on our behalf that he at last agreed to our appearance. He attended our rehearsal in a state of some *Anxiety*, which, despite all our skill and our professional demeanour, we seemed unable to Relieve; the poor man simply could not reconcile himself to the idea of a *Pig* upon his stage.

We had the happiness to prove him wrong, for we drew a full, indeed an *overflowing*, house, with a standing Ovation at the conclusion of our Act, and he afterwards came directly to us to offer his *Apologies*, and introduce us to his sister-in-law, the distinguished actress Mrs Siddons. I at first felt considerable trepidation in meeting that *Luminous* woman, whose piercing gaze seemed to penetrate one's very Soul — but as soon as we met, she laughed, and Curtsied, and told me she had a very good Report of me from her good friend Miss Seward, which gracious lady had written to her on my Account! It turned out to be *her* urging, and not Mr Dibdin's, that had secured us a place there, a kindness for which I at once expressed my undying gratitude. And, indeed, I later received from my dear Patroness a poem in her praise, which has been very well received, and which begins,

> SIDDONS, when first commenc'd thy
>   ardent course,
> The powers that guard the Drama's
>   aweful shrine,
> Beauty, and grandeur, tenderness, and
>   force,
> Silence that speaks, and eloquence
>   divine!

All of which, I can personally avouch, is *true*.

The next morning we breakfasted at our Inn, then made our way through the narrow streets of that ancient *City*, pausing at the foot of the deeply shadowed edifice of the Castle, at a place yet known as 'Hanging Corner'. Here, hard against a stone wall and a fortified Turret, stood an enormous Scaffold of dark wood, untenanted for the present, but ever ready to receive new *Visitors.* And, though it may indeed be said that its 'frame outlasts a thousand tenants', it is yet still true that the gallows does well by doing *ill*. No Animal but *Man* could, I aver, have ever conceived of such a structure, whose entire motive force is directed to the mechanical Extinguishment of a Life. Every other creature of the Earth knows, and all too well, that time on Earth is measured, and that many a *Rascal* may outlive a goodly creature, but Man alone presumes to take Fortune's very *Wheel* in his hands, and break it over the head of his Fellows.

And so we went upon our way, passing through the villages of Carnforth, Lowgill and Oddendale, making our next rest in the ancient town of Penrith, with its lovely market-square and ruined castle, where it was said that Richard III lived for some years prior to ascending — if that is the right word for it — the throne of England. Of course I knew him as a villain, and an especially cruel one, from Shakespeare, but I could not help but feel a measure of empathy for a man so often mocked for mere physical deformity — after all, there's 'no beast so fierce but knows some touch of pity' — even if the soul within were *more* deformed. The castle was built of handsome reddish stones, and was by way of slowly returning to the soil, as these same stones appeared in many a local dwelling or patch of wall, there being no other materials so near at hand in such a desolate country.

Of the hinterlands and frontiers that lie between England and Scotland, I can say but little, other than that — should the *Union* of these two countries be ever hoped to come to meaningful Fruition — it will first be necessary to improve the Roads. The zigzag passage of our wagon over hill and Dale, along the rutted, mad-angled and treacherous by-ways that pass for roads in these parts, made me more Sea-sick than ever I was aboard a ship. It was fortunate indeed that we had no engagements in this part of the country, as I would scarcely have been able to Stand, let alone give any kind of Performance, so greatly was I troubled in my Legs and afflicted in my Stomach. It was with a sense of blessed relief that we began our slow descent into the welcoming valley of the Clyde, and could glimpse at last, upon the Horizon, the sooty towers and busy quays of Glasgow, where next we were to make our Appearance.

We shortly crossed over the river and proceeded to King Street, where we arrived momentarily at our destination, the Dancing establishment of Mr *Frazer.* It was said, at the time of our Exhibition there, to be the principal school of Etiquette and fine Manners in the *City,* and very much the

Glass of Fashion for its inhabitants. One might wonder that such a place would welcome the presence of a Pig such as I, but on our meeting Mr Frazer all our uncertainty as to his motives was at a stroke *Dissolved.* Here was a man so jovial, so Warm of spirit, and yet so graceful in his manners, that he could manage to Roar with laughter without in the least way deviating from his excellent Deportment; indeed, he made the sound so freely and spontaneously, that he readily *Infected* all the Company around him with it. (I must here confess that, try though I might, I could not — nor could any of my Race — manage to emulate the human *Laugh,* but under Mr Frazer's influence and tutelage, I came as near such a Sound as I should ever hope to venture, convulsed as I was with a sort of intermittent Wheeze.)

Our host had made arrangements for our accommodation at an Inn convenient to the place, and on our arrival we found that all was paid for in advance, an act of kindness Rare among his kind. We had been engaged for a full week of double performances, with afternoon and evening shows each day, but both were of a different kind from any to which we had previously been accustomed. Mr Frazer had us in a front room on the ground floor, with a bay window facing the street, through which we could be seen as our own Advertisement. We did not, however, do any of our more complicated routines, but rather, on the hour and the half-hour, a sort of brief impromptu sketch, in which we took advantage of the composition of the Crowd and displayed some business fitted to their interests and Capacity. For children, we did simple sums and took questions on school subjects; for a crowd of women, we did an abbreviated version of our mind-reading act; for men, who were more abundant at the evening performance, we did our more elaborate routines, including Latin conjugations and declensions.

As the week progressed, I could see the wisdom of our Host's design: the shorter, periodic performances drew crowds into his antechambers, but also left them with idle time between our Acts — time in which, as it would happen, they might have a peep into one of the Dancing-rooms, and perhaps — especially if a young person were present with a parent or chaperone — they might enrol their names as pupils. I am sure that, during our sojourn there, we brought about a great increase in Business to Mr Frazer, much more than he was paying for our appearances; I might indeed have resented the

Bargain, save that I soon came quite to prefer these small and Spontaneous routines to our usual lengthier and more constrained ones. With them, I felt much more like a Visitor or a *Guest* than a mere Novelty or object of Admiration, and I was able to make the acquaintance of quite a number of the better sort of persons of the Town. Among these I might mention the painter Archibald Blair, the barrister John Orr, and the skilled instrument-maker and mathematician Murray *Ofburn,* all of whom paid me the most generous compliments, and with whom I enjoyed the pleasantest conversations.

Indeed, as the end of our time in Glasgow drew near, I found myself regretting our imminent departure — but I could not disappoint Dr Cullen, though it pained me to make my reconcilement to such a sad necessity. On our final Evening, the dancing hall was Cleared, and a stage erected so that I might give a full-scale Farewell performance, and the room was filled to overflowing. We brought back to the bill our Clairvoyant act, our *Whist,* and our 'Animal Magnetism' business, and finished the night with a grand Ball, followed by a dancing contest, for which I was given an honorary appointment as one of the Judges, a duty I discharged (I hope) quite capably, though my view of the dancers was perhaps not so *Elevated* as that of my fellow jurists. At the end, the winning couple was presented with a Cake, and I was given a laurel Wreath, aptly fitted to my Head, as a parting gift from a Committee of Leading Glaswegians — as a consequence of which, I have ever since styled myself the Pig *Laureate* of that fair City.

When compared with our previous turbulent journey, the turnpike from Glasgow to Edinburgh was 'smooth sailing' all the way; it consisted chiefly of a wide and steady *Track,* with inns at regular intervals and small towns nestled among the many ridges and vales, that followed for a time the course of the *Clyde.* The names of the towns themselves were most quaint and curious: in the course of one single mile we passed through the settlements of Sallysburgh, Threeprig and Kirk O'Shotts. Many of these consisted of no more than a cottage or two and a heap of stones; others of more substance managed a small inn, a Well, and a modest church or 'kirk', as they are called thereabouts; the most substantial had their own High Street, crowded with rows of old half-timbered houses and sometimes a small market-square.

Our progress was brisk, as we were most anxious to arrive at the appointed date, and by the afternoon of our third day, we could spy out the distant mass of Edinburgh *Castle,* which as we drew nearer seemed to stand almost alone atop its stony Cliffs, with the city itself a huddled, darker mass upon the horizon to its side. It made a sight most Dramatic, and one which I often recall with great Pleasure, as it marked the very first time I beheld that ancient yet lively citadel of Life and Learning, in which I have since made my Home.

We approached by way of Queensferry Road, which twisted and turned in slow ascent, and then became Lothian Road. From there, we diverged on to Castle Terrace, which went round the southern edge of Castle Rock itself, then passed by the King's Stables (so called) into the crowded thoroughfares of the *Grassmarket.* This district had many of the qualities of a typical market-square, save that it was extended in length as far as Twenty lesser such markets. Both sides of this vast swathe were crowded with shops, public houses, and sundry places of business, while in the middle area, a continuously shifting strip of tents and booths wound its way, looking for all the world like some Arabian bazaar, overflowing with goods and attractions of every describable sort. In the midst of all this clamour, fast by an ancient Well, stood yet another of those dark reminders of Human ways, a Gallows — I was relieved to learn that the last person to suffer upon it, one James *Andrews,* had been laid to rest, and the structure was shortly to be Removed for ever. I later discovered, to my great disappointment, that this was only on account of a *New* gallows having been erected within the city *Gaol* — evidence, to my mind, that there was at least some sense of *Shame* about the practice, though only enough to drive it indoors and away from Public view.

Much more to my liking were the tales told of the many showfolk who had there accomplished feats of great Fame, as in 1733 when a pair of Italians, father and son, strung a single rope from the battlements of the Castle to the south side of the *Market,* down which they slid, willy-nilly, first the father and then the son, the latter managing to blow continuously upon a Trumpet as he made his descent. Three days later, they staged another performance, with this addition: that after his descent, the father walked back up the rope all the way to the Castle walls, firing a pistol, beating a drum and loudly proclaiming that, while up there, he could defy the whole Court of Session!

Yet despite the lively history of the place, and our forthcoming Engagement to put on afternoon performances, we did not pause at any of the venerable Inns in those parts, having been advised by Dr Cullen that these were mostly very low houses, such that even those who stabled their horses there took rooms elsewhere if they could afford to. We proceeded instead to George-street, where that good man had arranged for us to stay in private lodgings not far from his own residence, and convenient to the hall of the College of Physicians. On our arrival, we were escorted to our rooms, which we found had been specially fitted with both a feather bed and one of Straw, with all the accoutrements of the latter laid out for my Convenience — among them a low table and basin, a brush and towel, and even a Mirror placed so that I might easily examine myself within it. Indeed, this was the first time since our early days at Mr Bisset's singular residence that I had ever had the sensation of being truly at Home, in a place where both my stature and capabilities were perfectly accommodated.

That very evening, Dr Cullen came to

meet us, and made us feel twice welcome with his easy demeanour and natural manners. Given the length of our journey, he was most anxious that we felt no obligation to make any appearances, or greet any new or strange *Faces,* before we were able to take our Rest. During the course of his visit, our dinner was brought to us by a young serving-boy of the name of *Jamie* — who has since become a fast friend — while we discussed our future plans and possibilities. My engagement in the Grassmarket, which commenced three days hence, was to be strictly limited to a fortnight, and was advertised as 'the very Final Appearance of that Famous Pig, TOBY, whose remarkable skill with *Language* exceeds that of any of his Rivals, and has been the subject of Universal acclamation in Dublin, London, Glasgow and numerous other places throughout the British Isles'. Once I had taken my last Bow, however, my plans were far less certain: I had considered retiring to a place in the Country, a tour of Europe (purely as a Spectator, not a Performer), or perhaps undertaking a voyage to *America.*

Dr Cullen nodded attentively as I spelt out my Options, and commended me on my abiding interest in the world about me — but then he paused, looking upon me with a strange, yet benevolent gaze.

'Toby, you are a most remarkable fellow; would that I had among my students any with half your intelligence and native curiosity! I have heard that you had completed scarcely a Year of your studies, and that your removal to London, and the subsequent death of Dr Adams, prevented you from resuming them. You must know that I have most carefully considered what I am about to say, and would not make the offer were it not both in my power and Approved by all the requisite authorities. So I say to you, would you like to be a student here at the University? Ours may not be so ancient as the halls of *Oxford,* but we have built here as strong a fortress of Learning as any they have there. Our lectures, our Libraries and our tutors would be at your disposal, and you would be Registered as my pupil, with all the privileges and responsibilities of any other student here. What say you? Will you not consider it?'

I hesitated only a moment — and that because I was utterly overcome by the generosity of his offer — before I at once spelt out my acceptance of this singular Honour. I could think of no way to thank him; I was sure I had not been of any special service — nor did I know of any other

Friends who might have advocated on my behalf.

'But what about the matter of Fees?' I asked, with some trepidation.

'You have more friends than you may realise; I myself raised a subscription among them, and from my colleagues here in Edinburgh, and from these funds all such sums will be paid, as well as an allowance for room, board and any books or other supplies you may require.'

To this astonishing news I could make no reply — I simply bowed low.

17

But before my studies could commence, I had one last performance to give, and I was determined that it should be my best. Sam and I had engaged a local carpenter to erect for us a spacious, purpose-built Booth, quite nearly the size of a small house, at the best pitch on the Grassmarket, just adjacent to the West Port, past which nearly everyone and everything passed on its way to or from market. Incorporated into this was a large banner, boldly painted on a length of tautly stretched linen, which depicted scenes from my entire Life and Career, under the following heads, *viz.,* 'Toby is born at SALFORD'; 'Toby at Astley's Amphitheatre, DUBLIN'; 'Toby a pupil at OXFORD'; 'Triumph in LONDON'; and finally 'Elected Pig-laureate at GLASGOW'. We engaged two subsidiary showmen as 'barkers' to drum up business at either end of the market, and a small fleet of boys to serve as animated *Sandwiches,* parading through town between two slabs of wood upon which were plastered the Bills for our show. Notices in all the papers completed the plan of our Campaign; never, to my knowledge, has any such show been more widely *Advertis'd* in advance of its Opening.

Given the means employed, we expected a goodly crowd, and we were not disappointed; indeed, the numbers so greatly exceeded our expectations that we were obliged to add a third, and later a *fourth,* Show every day. Eager crowds of local citizenry queued long before our first appearance each day at Noon, and well after our final show each evening, the disappointed mingled with the men who were busy removing the market-stalls and unsold produce. The notices in the local papers were exceedingly kind, and each night in our lodgings we were presented with further letters and notes addressed to me, offering warm tributes to my work, and enquiring about tickets for the next Performance. By the third day, our morning stroll to the Grassmarket became a sort of Procession, with the local crossing-sweepers and errand-boys proclaiming our progress and heralding our Entry, as though we were *Royalty,* while behind us trailed a string of carts, cos- termongers and carriages nearly as extensive as the Lord Mayor's Parade in *London.*

A few days into our run, I received a singular *Visitor,* a man whose Star was just then most Ascendant in the Sky: Robert *Burns,* the Ayrshire ploughman-turned-poet. He arrived in fine fettle, in the company of Mr Creech, a local bookseller who had just then undertaken to publish a new edition of his Poems, along with a large gaggle of miscellaneous *Followers,* whose exact con- nection with the Poet was hard to Ascertain. They made, never the less, for a most colourful audience, and Sam at once ar- ranged for them to be seated together, and issued tickets *gratis,* which would have of- fended those yet waiting to attend had it been any other person but *Burns.* The great poet himself, remarkably, seemed unaf- fected by this adulation: he retained a sturdy rustic dignity which seemed to regard all Praise as superfluous; his countenance pos- sessed at all times a constant, even Tempera- ment, and it was only in his *eyes* that there glimmered — or so I thought — an intensity of Feeling that belied his modest appear- ance and calm comportment. Truly, I have never beheld a pair of eyes such as those,

before or since, and when — at the conclusion of my performance — we were introduced, I felt myself quite under their Spell.
We exchanged only bows and polite glances,
but I am sure I was not alone in sensing a
strange feeling of kinship between us, these
two simple Country creatures whose capacity for Language was similarly made out to
be some remarkable *Spectacle,* eliciting
adulation that would somehow be lessened
had we both been born not Sons of *Toil* but
to a gentler class.

This feeling was renewed, some time later,
when I heard from Dr Cullen that Mr
Burns, invited to a fashionable *soirée* by a
Countess, where he feared he would be
greeted not as a true Friend but rather a
mere Curiosity, had replied thusly: 'Mr
Burns will do himself the honour of waiting
upon her on the ninth inst., provided Her
Ladyship will also invite the Learned Pig.'
This has, since then, been interpreted as far
from complimentary, by a great many
ignorant and idle commentators who have
supposed that for Burns to compare himself
to *Me* was a reflection of a perceived Insult,
rather than — as I am sure it was meant —
a most generous avowal of our abiding sense
of kinship. Poor Burns: though the span of
life granted Man is (generally) many times

that allotted to *Pigs,* he had scarce another nine years of life, while I have lived to mourn his Death, and regret the brevity, though not the brilliance, of his poetic Career.

As for myself, the remainder of my performances in the Grassmarket were as great a success as the first, and I was then, and have for ever since been, grateful to the people of *Edinburgh* for the accolades and attendance with which I was showered for the duration of my Show. On the final evening, it was attended by the Lord Provost, Sir James Stirling, accompanied by a great many councillors of that fair City; there was also a delegation from the University, which included Dr Cullen, along with his estimable colleague Dr Monro, and the poet and playwright John *Home,* who paid me the singular compliment of reading an *Encomium* he had composed for the occasion, which concluded,

Where next may lie the Realms you will
   explore,
When Science to you opens all her store?
Already have you in your sapient brain
More than most men in all their lives
   attain!

> May we not hope, in this improving Age
> Of human things — to see on Terra's
>   stage
> Pigs take the lead of men, and from their
>   styes
> To honours, riches, and high office, rise!

I thanked him much for that, although I was taken aback by the strange vision it painted of a world of Porcine attainments — for myself, as for my Fellows, I was sure that we wanted only to be left to our own Devices, and would count ourselves fortunate to live out our lives untroubled by human *Affairs* — but his intention was so clearly generous that I said nothing of it.

Following the conclusion of my final performance, and after taking innumerable Bows, I processed with my friends to the northern side of the Grassmarket, where the crowd divided and dispersed into the several public Houses located there: some to the White *Hart,* some to the Black *Bull,* and some — Sam and myself included — to the Bee Hive *Inn,* which had become our favoured place of resort. As I have already mentioned, I never partake of spirituous liquors or Ales, but the manager of this place was so very Kind and accommodating that he himself often took the trouble to bring me a pail of cold porridge in-between my performances. He and Sam had become fast friends, and we would often, in company with Dr Cullen and others of our Edinburgh acquaintance, gather there at the end of the day. That evening, we were the Toast of the Town, and it was late indeed before the last of the revellers who desired to Drink to my *Health* departed, and Sam and I could at last have a moment to ourselves.

In the calm retreat of our corner table, with no sound other than that of the proprietor washing out the stoups, the world seemed almost *too* quiet, and I wondered whether I would miss the sound of Applause, and the noise of a crowd astounded at my feet. It gave me a curious feeling to *Reflect* on my long career upon the Stage, whence I had been thrust at such a Tender age, that I could scarcely imagine a life without it. To most who have lived their entire lives in the Public Eye, such a thought may well seem *Impossible,* for they have come to feel fully alive only in the glow of those delightful *Beams* of adulation, the loss of which would bring on a fearful Darkness. And yet I was unlike them: an *Actor* may play many parts, however briefly he struts upon the Stage; a *Musician* can learn to play other sorts of Songs; a *Conjuror* is always learning and perfecting new Tricks, as an *Acrobat* new stunts and routines — whereas my one real *Act* was my mere Existence, and my demonstration extended only so far as to prove that I possessed those capacities common in Man, but so rare among *Pigs.* Thus I reasoned that, for me, the retirement from my theatrical role was — in a manner profound and strange — never really possible: whether Reading at my leisure, attending a Lecture, or simply patching a torn spot on my Waistcoat, whether seen by a crowd or by a single *Observer,* I was, so long as I lived, condemned to a sort of *Perpetual* display. Truly, for me, all the world *was* a stage, and there could be no exit from the latter, until I departed the Former.

This given, I reflected, I would, by pursuing my studies, at least improve my private capacity for enjoyment, whereas to make any alteration in my outward life would be far more difficult. Indeed, there was only one manner in which I could shuffle off my status as a Freak of Nature, and it was the one thing I dreaded most: to shed my singularity and return to the common multitude of pigs, *sans* education, *sans* waistcoat and — ultimately — *sans* self. So, from that time forward, I resolved to devote myself to study, and to learning as much as was possible, given the more modest span of life allotted my *Race*.

And so my learning began in *Earnest*. Through the kindness of Dr Cullen, I removed to a small room in a building directly adjoining the Surgeons' Hall. From there, without assistance, I could navigate the corridors that would bring me to Lecture-hall and Library, and — by means of a small Lift or 'dumb-waiter' — descend to the ground floor, and thence make my way to any of the neighbouring buildings. Of the fact that I could manage all this on my own, I was justly proud but, never the less, Dr Cullen insisted that Jamie be lodged in an adjoining room, and ready to assist me whenever I required it — and to this I consented, for he was as kind-hearted and reliable a lad as any I had known; he reminded me very much of *Sam* when he was younger, save that when he Spoke his words came out in softly bristled Scots brogue.

Being under the immediate tutelage of Dr Cullen, I began with a course in Chemistry, of which he was past professor; the current holder of that Chair, Mr Joseph Black, was a good friend of his and proved a ready teacher. I attended his Lectures twice weekly, as well as attending his Tutorials, in company with several other Undergraduates, in his chambers, which were just down the hallway from my Own. At the same time, I undertook a course in Natural History under Professor *Walker,* another close colleague of my mentor's. This difficult and extensive Subject was carried forth over both terms, moving from *Meteorology, Hydrology* and *Geology* in the first, to *Minerals, Plants* and, finally, *Animals* in the second half of the year. I was thus obliged to save my favourite subject for Last, but I was not disappointed: Professor Walker was, by that time, sufficiently impressed with my Abilities that he proposed revising the entire Taxonomy of *Linnaeus,* removing Pigs entirely from the family *Bestiae* and placing them alongside Man in a new grouping, *Animaloe rationis,* which I felt showed a remarkable insight and ability to adapt to new Knowledge.

In the year following, I studied Literature and *Belles Lettres* with Professor William Greenfield, successor to the brilliant Hugh Blair, by whose work the reputation of this fairly *novel* field of Enquiry had been very much advanced. Alongside this, I pursued the subject of Moral Philosophy with Dugald Stewart. Stewart was a far harder man to please: his entire course concerned the 'moral powers of man', and he was quite bitterly disinclined to so much as acknowledge my presence in the lecture-hall. From his tutorials I was utterly excluded, and it was only through the offices of a kindly fellow-student that I was able to obtain notes of these meetings, which enabled me to pass his course. He held throughout to his view that 'animals, considered individually, discover but a small degree of sagacity', although he was latterly persuaded to add that they 'make some small acquisitions by experience, as sufficiently appears, in certain tribes, from the sagacity of old, when contrasted with the ignorance of the young; and from the effects which may be produced on at least *some* of them, by discipline and education'. I like to think that it was on *My* account that he added this last sentence, but our relations, alas, were never as cordial as those with my other Professors.

At last, these courses of my education Done, I was ready to sit for my examinations, and apply for matriculation as a Bachelor of *Arts*. In preparation, I did much as my human fellows did, burning the 'midnight oil' in great quantities, and taking part with several of my fellow-students in the mock-examinations and Interrogations with which we did our best to anticipate our final Test. Finally, the day came, and I was very nearly in a Panic, when I found that the Hall where the examinations were to be held could only be entered by a very steep flight of Steps, which it surpassed the ability of my short legs to Ascend. I could not help thinking of poor Dr Johnson in his last *Infirmity,* unable to enter the Bodleian — and then, just as I was on the Precipice of Despair, there was Jamie to help me *Up.* I took my place in the very back row just as the great Bell rang, which announced that the doors must be closed. As had been previously arranged, I had a special *Examiner* to give me my questions, who then transcribed my answers, which I spelt out as fast as ever I could. It took me until the very instant of the closing bell, by which time I was quite overcome with Nervous exhaustion, and barely able to waddle out of the Hall.

I slept for nearly fourteen Hours that night, with (or so I was later told) both Sam and Jamie ministering at my side, concerned for my safety in such a State — but Dr Cullen reassured them that such a Rest was entirely natural, given my circumstances. When I awoke, I was at first quite groggy as to my surroundings, and it seemed to me that the faces of my Friends only gradually emerged out of a veritable Porridge of blurred and fragmented Forms. After taking a small Breakfast, I felt at once *Revived,* as if I had been recalled, Lazarus-like, from the Realms of the Dead, and took a stroll out upon the Balcony, which overlooked the great City of Edinburgh with all its wide Environs. Whatever might come next, I resolved then and there that I would Remain here, in the midst of this vast and variegated City from which I had received my greatest Welcome.

The very next day, I was visited at an unusually early Hour by no less than Dr Cullen himself. In his hand he held a be-ribboned Scroll, which I knew must contain the results of my Examination, for which I trembled in my very Soul. It was not for Myself that I feared — I would get on well enough, with or without any great *Credentials* — but for my Friends, who had laboured so dearly on my Behalf, and granted me such an array of Advantages, that I would be very deeply ashamed to *Disappoint* them. I quickly took up my letters, and spelt out my fearful query:
H-A-V-E I P-A-S-S-E-D.
'Have you passed?' echoed Dr Cullen. 'My

dear Toby, you must know that we could not hold you in any higher Regard, whatever the result of your examination. But here I must tell you that the Result of your efforts has been something so Unusual that I scarcely know how to communicate it.'

U-N-U-S-U-A-L, I spelt, with excruciating slowness.

'Toby, according to the Examiners for Degrees in the Faculty of Arts, you have earned not only a passing mark, and not only the designation *primi ordinis,* but the highest score of your entire class, entitling you to the degree of Bachelor of Arts *cum laude.'*

They tell me that, upon receipt of this News, I suddenly *Fainted,* but I can only relate that when I Awoke, some uncertain time later, I was by any measure the happiest Pig on *Earth.*

18

It has been some years now since the experiences recorded in the precedent pages, and although in that time my travels have been entirely of the *Interior* variety, I am confident that they have been just as extensive — if not more so — than any I undertook in my early days as a peripatetic Pig, for whom the *Road* was more home than any settled place. *Musco lapis volutus haud obvolvitur,* as Publilius Syrus says — moss covers not the moving stone! — but a great deal can be gained without the least *Motion,* though moss may have its day. In the years that have followed my journeys, I have had both time and *Cause* for reflection, both upon my own life and the far stranger Lives of the creatures I have found myself among — those known as *'Homo sapiens'* — that is, reasoning Man — or, as Dean Swift far more

wisely preferred, *'Homo rationis capax'* —
man *capable* of Reason, but who all too
often eschews his capacity and revels in his
own *Filth* far more deeply than he supposes
Pigs do.

Having completed my degree at the University of Edinburgh, I thought myself as
capable, if not more so, than any Man in
comprehending the ways of this wide and
Troublesome world, in which so great a portion of Things to come is left to *Chance.* I
read, of course, the daily papers, but took
most pleasure in continuing my Literary
and Philosophical studies, within which I
discovered many of the curious mechanisms
of Man, which are devoted (if I may say so)
far more to making his actions *seem* reason-
able, than to actually making them so. I
travelled widely in the works of Hobbes,
and sojourned with Swift in his *Gulliverian*
mode; with Pope I devoured his Essay on
Man, and accompanied Smollett on the road
in company with Peregrine *Pickle* and
Humphry *Clinker.*

But the most Curious and unexpected
Book I ever encountered never came from
the Pens of these famous Wits. I had at the
time a standing Order with *Creech's,* to
bring for my review any Works of note new
imprinted in England, Scotland or Wales,

which might bear upon my *Interests*. Atop
this pile one day I was stunned to discover
a new Book, which shamelessly proclaimed
itself *My* autobiography! Boldly entitled *The
Life and Adventures of Toby the SAPIENT PIG,
with his Opinions on Men and Manners,* this
spurious compendium made sport of its
Subject, subjecting me to the most Ridiculous impositions imaginable: that my
Mother had gained her 'knowledge' by eating a portion of her master's Library; that I
had in my 'previous lives' been incarnated
as a dog, a scorpion, and even a Fly; that
even my name was a corruption of 'to be or
not to be' — and more. The author of this
treatise, indeed, could not resist a Pun,
declaring my favourite play to be *Hamlet,*
my favourite authors 'Hogg' and 'Bacon',
and so forth. Most incredibly of all, this
portmanteau Porker had the audacity to
declaim against the distortions of the *Press:*
'They twisted me badly, some of the edi-
tors; from what they wrote, I firmly believe
they had never been there.'

It was the receipt of this pamphlet — for
it was really no more than that — which
persuaded me at last that I must write my
own Memoirs, if only to set forth clearly
and without scurrilous embellishment the
actual transit of my Career. Indeed, as I

foresaw that my time upon earth was drawing near its Close, I feared, as did that noble *Dane,* 'what a wounded name, things standing thus unknown, shall live behind me!' And so I set forth to un-wound, and unwind my Life, a project to which I was uniquely suited. Sam and I had retained copies of all of our Bills, along with the notices from the Papers, which we kept in several large scrap-books; these were the only aid to Memory that I sought, or needed, besides a copy of that one invaluable reference, Laurie and Whittle's *New and Improved English Atlas, Divided into Counties,* which I do not hesitate to recommend to anyone who is recalling, or planning, a long Journey.

My principal assistant throughout was Jamie, who had some time since grown into a strapping young Man, but who maintained himself with me throughout my declining years. I should mention that Sam, just as he had at Oxford, was also able to attend the University, becoming at first a Bachelor and later a *Master* of Arts, and eventually opening a small country School, for the education of less fortunate Children than himself. I often visited him there, and on occasion, at the demand of the Children, would put on a small performance, the only ones I ever did after my official 'retirement' from the Stage. Having Jamie enabled me to carry on my work, and Sam to live his own Life, a change that, though distressing in some respects, was both Necessary and Beneficial to us Both.

For the purpose of composing such a lengthy text, cards were far too cumbersome; instead, I invented a *Device,* in form much like a large pasteboard clock-face, whose 'hands' I could direct at the letters and numbers ranged round its circumference. By grouping the most common letters, such as E, T, A and O, together near the point of Noon, and far less frequently employed ones — X, J, Q and Z — towards six o'clock, I obtained remarkable speed and efficiency, and could quite frequently manage several pages a day. These Jamie transcribed into a large bound ledger, whence he later made a Fair Copy, for delivery to my Publishers. Thus equipped, my Literary progress was completed in just under a Year, and brought out by Creech that same November, whence it has received the kind of warm, widespread Interest and Acclaim that I could scarcely have Hoped for it. As for the Specious narrative penned by that 'other' Toby, it has proven to be a mere passing Novelty, quite washed away with the Tide of the true and *Correct* story of my Life, and I can only hope that in years to come, it will entirely be Forgotten.

The hope that one's inner spirit may be Captured in language, like a fly in Amber, perpetually present even after its Owner has taken leave of his material body, is a very old one. Plato, as I recall — or perhaps it was Socrates: my memory has grown rather cloudy — discerns a *Difference* between our 'mortal' children, that, is, our Offspring, and our 'immortal' ones, which are our Ideas. Of course, not *everyone*'s ideas can last for ever, and one may recall that even Plato once inveighed against the art of *Writing,* which he feared would diminish our Capacity for Memory. Yet it is only because his declamation was *written down* that we have any idea of it; the world of those Ancient Greeks is long gone, with Ruins immemorial in its place. So therefore it is my hope that, once my own *Carcass* has, as is very likely, returned into the Sod whence it sprang, leaving only a small scattering of Bones, these my words, and this my *Story,* which you now hold in your hands, will live on.

FINIS

NARRATIVE

Given in order of their first appearance, and with historical notes by the present editor, along with glosses of the Latin words and phrases.

Mr Francis *Lloyd.* It would be immensely gratifying to know the exact place of TO-BY's birth. However, although the inscription 'Boothes Hall' appears on some old maps, there does not seem to be any certain record of Mr Francis Lloyd. The name itself was quite common: a Francis Lloyd was a member of the House of Commons in 1692; another was Rector of Trottesclive (now Trottiscliffe, Kent) in 1759; yet another was said to be a manufacturer in London *c.* 1830 — he had a son, Julius, who became Rector of St Philip, Salford, in 1891 — which is as close as the name can be placed to our *hero,* albeit it comes a century too late.

Samuel *Nicholson.* Information about Mr Nicholson is, alas, very scattered, and we are obliged to rely on fragmentary accounts. In his book *Learned Pigs and Fireproof Women* (1986), Ricky Jay offers the most extensive account: he states that in 1784 Mr Nicholson appeared in London with a troupe of Animals nearly identical with those of the late Mr Bisset; he also recounts TOBY's appearance at the Academy Room in the Lyceum in 1786, as well as his 'Scottish Tour'. Jan Bondeson, in her book *The Feejee Mermaid and other Essays in Natural and Unnatural History* (1999), says only that 'Mr Bisset's pig was taken over by a certain Mr Nicholson, about whose previous career little is known'; he also describes the first leg of his northern tour (though he later confuses him with his rival at Sadler's Wells), and notes that he 'surfaced' in Edinburgh in late 1787, where he was seen by Robert Burns.

None of this is entirely satisfactory: we have neither a definite time nor place of birth, nor any notion of his career before or after his association with TOBY. We are left with only glimpses, as in this account from the *Glasgow Mercury*:

Among the infinite number of curiosities hitherto offered to the inspection and attention of the public, there are none which lay so great a claim to our attention and approbation as the wonderful and astonishing performances of

266

the 'learned pig' now exhibiting in Mr Frazer's Dancing Hall, King Street, from eleven o'clock, forenoon, to three in the afternoon, and from five to nine at night, where it may be seen this and every day in the ensuing week, at the expiration of which the proprietor is under engagement to set off for Edinburgh.

This most singular phenomenon is one of the many surprising instances of the ingenuity of Mr Nicholson — a man who is possessed of an exclusive and peculiar power over the most irrational part of animated nature. Many of the first personages in the three kingdoms have been witnesses to his persevering temper and patience in the tuition of beasts, birds, etc., in a degree that has seldom fallen to the lot of human infirmity. As to his Pig, this singular creature may justly be deemed the greatest curiosity in the kingdom, and the proprietor makes no doubt but he will give that satisfaction, and receive that approbation, from the ladies and gentlemen of this city, &c., &c., which he has done in London and Edinburgh.

As to the later career of Mr Nicholson, we possess only the most slender evidence;

although the records of the University of Edinburgh confirm that he studied there, there appears to be no record of his having taken a degree at the time. Regarding the country school that he is said to have established, we have only TOBY's account. And yet, curiously, there is a record of one 'Samuel Nicholson' receiving a medical qualification at Edinburgh in September of 1835; we can only suppose that this may have been a son or perhaps even a grandson.

Mr Silas *Bisset*
It should be noted that there is some uncertainty in the historical record as to Mr Bisset's given name: during his lifetime, his name was most often printed as 'S. Bisset', and later sources give both Silas and *Samuel* (the latter due to confusion with Mr *Nicholson*). By far the most extensive account of Mr Bisset's life and career is that related by Henry Wilson in his collection *Wonderful characters: comprising memoirs and anecdotes of the most Remarkable Persons of Every Age and Nation, Collected from the most authentic sources,* (1821); Wilson sums up Bisset's career thus:

Perhaps no period ever produced a more singular character than Bisset; though in the age of apathy in which he lived, his merit was but little rewarded. At any former era of time, the man who could assume a command over dumb creation, and make them act with a docility which far exceeded mere brutal instinct, would have been looked upon as possessed of supernatural powers, according to the pagan notions; or would have been burned as a wizard, according to the Christian system.

Wilson states that Bisset was born at Perth, Scotland, about the year 1721, and had originally worked as a shoemaker in London. He hit upon the 'notion of teaching quadrupeds' later in life, after reading an account of a remarkable horse, which had appeared at the fair of St Germain's. His first trials were said to be with dogs, and 'two monkies [*sic*] were the next pupils he took in hand'; then came hares, canaries, linnets, the infamous turkeys, and even a goldfish (though what this fish was taught to do is left to the reader's imagination). Bisset's association with TOBY is said to have been a response to a sort of challenge: 'A doubt being stated to him, whether the obstinacy of a pig could be conquered, his usual patient fortitude was practised to try the experiment; in the course of sixteen months, he made an animal, supposed the most obstinate and perverse in nature, to become the most tractable and docile.'

Wilson mentions Bisset's appearance in Dublin, and briefly describes the incident with the nameless constable:

Bisset was thus in a fair way of bringing his pig to a good market when a Constable, whose ignorance and insolence disgraced his authority, broke into the room; with that brutality which the idea of power gives (what Shakespeare calls) a 'pelting petty officer', he assaulted the unoffending man, broke and destroyed every thing by which the performance was directed, and drew his sword to kill the swine, which might justly have been called a half-reasoning, instead of a grovelling animal, that in the practice of good manners, was at least the superior of the assailant. The injured Bisset pleaded, without any avail, the permission he obtained from the chief magistrate; he was threatened to be dragged to prison, if he was found any more offending in the same manner.

This account agrees in nearly every particular with that of TOBY, save that the incident with the Constable is supposed to have happened in Dublin, a very slight discrepancy when all other details are considered.

Finally, we have an Obituary notice from a Chester newspaper, which confirms his death there, and the high estimate of his abilities he earned in that city:

Last week at Chester the celebrated Mr S. BISSET, the most remarkable man that probably ever lived for cultivating an intimacy with the dumb creation. He made a figure in London several years ago, as conductor of the Cats Opera; since which time he has instructed, in the most curious tricks and deceptions, several dogs, horses, turtles, birds &c., and latterly a Pig, which was lately shewn in the North and in this city, and with which he was on his way to London when he died.

Mr James *Blackburn*, Mayor of LIVERPOOL. His name is given as 'James *Blackburn*, the Younger' in Liverpool records, where his occupation is listed as 'cloth manufacturer'. Little else appears to be known about the weave and weft of the man.

Astley's AMPHITHEATRE, Dublin. Philip *Astley* (8 January 1742–27 January 1814) is regarded by many as the 'father of the modern circus'. The concept of a 'circus', based around a circular riding track and featuring trick-riders along with interludes by acrobats, jugglers, rope-walkers and other entertainers, was inaugurated by Astley in London in 1768; it was later greatly expanded and enclosed in a purpose-built wooden structure. Flush with the success of this London establishment, Astley erected a second 'Amphitheatre' in Dublin in 1773, making use of the house and grounds formerly the residence of the Molyneux family in Peter Street; it was here that TOBY made his Dublin début.

Monsieur *Bussart,* Monsieur *Redigé,* Signor *Scaglioni, La Belle Espagnole, Herr Hautknochen.* The troupe is undoubtedly that of Alexandre Placide *Bussart* who, together with his wife, led a famous company of tightrope performers and dancers in the 1790s. He was said to have been the most graceful rope-dancer and gymnast of his day, performing with much success in both Paris and London. In 1792, he travelled with his company to the United States, where they performed before President

George Washington. In England, they often appeared with Monsieur Redigé, who was also known as the 'Little Devil'. A treatise of the time noted that 'At Sadler's *Wells*, the performances, other than music or dancing, consisted of posturing by a boy called the Infant Hercules, and tightrope dancing by Madame Romaine, another female artiste known as La Belle Espagnole, and two lads, one of whom was a son of Richer, the other known as the "Little Devil".' According to Richard Findlater's 1978 book *Joe Grimaldi, His Life and Theatre*, La Belle Espagnole did indeed dance 'with two swords tied to her feet, and two eggs under them, while she carried two baskets on a board', much as TOBY has described. As for Signor Scaglioni and his Dogs, we have a 1788 handbill from Salisbury which declares that,

On MONDAY, August 11, 1788, will be exhibited the real Original DANCING DOGS, And other ENTERTAIN-MENTS, Particularly the imitation of various Song Birds; likewise Singing, Dancing, and a variety of novel Amuse-ments, Under the Direction of Signor SCAGLIONI and Mr HERMAN. Boxes 2*s.* — Pit 1*s.* — Gallery 6*d.* The doors to be opened at half past six and begin at eight. Performances every evening this week, Saturday excepted.

Herr *Hautknochen,* whose stage-name is German for 'skin and bones', has not been identified.

Mr *Robinson* of the *Freeman's Journal.* The *Freeman's Journal,* founded in 1763 by Charles Lucas, began as a strident platform for Irish nationalism, but this changed in 1784 when Francis Higgins gained control of the paper, after which it took a decidedly pro-British stance. Mr *Robinson* has not been identified.

DRUMCONDRA, Mr *Bellows.* Drumcondra (Irish: *Droim Conrach,* meaning 'Conra's Ridge') is a residential area and inner suburb on the Northside of Dublin, Ireland. It is administered by Dublin City Council. The river Tolka and the Royal Canal flow through the area. The editor has visited the place, and its character is remarkably unaltered — though far more densely populated — from its state in TOBY's day. Mr *Bellows* has not been identified.

'The VAULTS', Belfast, Mr *Atkins.* According to John C. Greene, in his invaluable treatise *Theatre in Belfast: 1736–1800,* a theatre of this name opened in disused wine cellars in Belfast in 1731 under the management of a 'Mr Johnes'. There is some confusion as to the exact location of this venue, but in any case, according to Mr Greene's study, the last recorded performance was in 1766, which would mean that Toby's appearance there extends its known life by two decades or more. Mr *Atkins* is most likely the same man who was noted as the manager of the Belfast Theatre in 1785, when Mrs Siddons — whom TOBY was later to meet in Lancaster — visited Belfast and praised Mr Atkins for his 'probity and excellent management'. (George Benn, *A History of the Town of Belfast,* Vol. II).

The constable has not been identified.

Edward *Dobbs.* Mr *Dobbs* has proven difficult to identify. If we suppose him to have been long-lived, however, he may be identical with the man of that name awarded five pounds as the First Prize for 'Fat Pigs, not exceeding nine months old' in Birmingham in 1835 (*Farmer's Magazine,* Vol. 21).

THEATRE-ROYAL, Chester; Messrs *Banks* &

Ward, Mr Dawes. Michael Kelley, in his *Reminiscences of Michael Kelly, of the King's theatre, and Theatre royal* (1826), speaks of meeting '*Banks* and *Ward,* the proprietors of the Chester and Manchester Theatres'. Mr *Dawes* has not been identified.

Mrs Cowley's 'More Ways than One'. Hannah *Cowley* (14 March 1743–11 March 1809) was a successful English dramatist and poet. Legend has it that, on attending the theatre with her husband, she remarked to him that she could write as good a piece as the one being performed, and within a fortnight she had finished her first play, *The Runaway,* which was produced at Drury Lane by David Garrick in 1776. Many more followed, most notably *The Belle's Stratagem* in 1782, which was her most successful. *More Ways Than One,* the play within which TOBY's interlude was featured, had opened at Covent Garden in 1783 and was, at the time of our narrative, nearing the end of its subsequent provincial tour.

Mr *Edwin* as 'Sir Marvell *Mushroom*'. A 'Mr *Edwin*' is indeed mentioned in this role in the *dramatis personae* in the 1813 edition of the *Plays of Mrs Cowley;* he apparently appeared in many productions of her plays.

We have been unable to find out much else about him.

Sir William *Dunkinfield,* Baronet, High Sheriff of CHESHIRE. A person of this name held that office from 1751 to 1774; although he was (apparently) no longer Sheriff by the time his name was invoked by Mr Nicholson, he must have retained something of the mantle of that office, at least among the hoi-polloi.

ST GILES'S FAIR. *St Giles's Fair* is an annual fair held in St Giles, a wide thoroughfare in central north Oxford, in September of each year. It was, just as TOBY describes it, very much an affair of *town* and not of *gown.* Never the less, it has been warmly and richly recalled by at least one undergraduate, who in an essay for the *Magdalen College School Journal* described it thus:

> The next excitement is St Giles's FAIR, when the whole length of the street from the Church to the Martyr's Memorial is occupied by four rows of booths, tenanted by the fat woman, the thin child, the pig with two heads, and similar wonders; penny peepshows and roundabouts, waxworks and cake stalls, cheap-

jacks, 'theatres' and shooting galleries make up the rest. All the villagers round flock to this their holiday: infant Oxford devotes itself for a couple of days to gingerbread, drums and whistles; youthful Oxford gives itself up entirely to 'scratch-backs', weapons to which we, not being Scotchmen, have a decided objection; staider Oxford, who are above such trifles, retire to the public-house in the vicinity of the fair.

It should be noted that that description dates to some years after the present narrative, and to a time when — *learned* pigs being apparently no longer available — those with two heads were the best that could be obtained.

Dr William *Adams,* Master of PEMBROKE COLLEGE, *Oxon.* William *Adams* DD (*c.* 1706–13 January 1789) was Fellow and Master of Pembroke College, Oxford. A brief Life is given by Charles Partington in his *British Cyclopedia* of 1837:

Dr Adams was born at Shrewsbury, and at the age of thirteen was entered at Pembroke College, where he remained to take his master's degree, and obtained a fellowship. It has generally been reported that he was afterwards tutor to the celebrated Dr Johnson; but Dr Adams very handsomely contradicted this report, by saying that had Johnson returned to College after Jordan's (his tutor's) death, he might have been his tutor: 'I was his nominal tutor, but he was above my mark.'

In 1732, he obtained the curacy of St Chad's in Shrewsbury, and left the college. Never the less, when, forty-three years later, John Ratcliffe, master of Pembroke, died, Dr Adams was elected to take his place. His term commenced on 26 July 1775, and he presided over the college with universal approbation, earning the affections of the students by his courteous demeanour and affability, mixed with the firmness necessary for the preservation of discipline. In his apartments here, he frequently cheered the latter days of his old friend Dr Johnson, whom he survived but a few years; dying at his house at Gloucester, 13 January 1789, aged eighty-two. He was interred in Gloucester Cathedral, where a monument was erected, with an inscription celebrating his ingenuity, learning, eloquence, piety and benevolence.

It was doubtless to the fund for this last-mentioned memorial that TOBY contributed.

Dr Samuel *Johnson*. Samuel *Johnson* (18 September 1709 [OS 7 September]–13 December 1784), often referred to simply as 'Dr Johnson', was widely regarded as the most distinguished man of letters of his day. He is best known for his *Dictionary of the English Language,* published in 1755, as well as for his essays, poems and other writings, particularly the romance *Rasselas: Prince of Abyssinia* (1759), a copy of which TOBY tells us was among his most prized possessions. After a year as a student at Pembroke College, he was obliged to leave due to lack of funds just prior to Dr Adams's appointment as a Fellow; although they had not in fact been pupil and master, they never the less developed a strong friendship that lasted until Johnson's death.

During the time described in the book, Dr Johnson was in the throes of what was to be his final illness; he had recently undergone surgery for gout and had been confined to his bed for much of the latter part of 1783. By the summer of 1784, his condition seemed to have improved somewhat, and that season he made his final visit to Oxford, which gives a definite date to his appearance in the present narrative. That autumn, his health in rapid decline, Johnson expressed a desire to die in London and arrived there on 16 November. His final days were painful in the extreme, although he still managed at times to display his characteristic spirit; when his physician, Dr Warren, asked him in his usual manner whether he was feeling better, Johnson replied, 'No, Sir; you cannot conceive with what acceleration I advance towards death.' He was buried at Westminster Abbey in 'Poets' Corner', not far from the graves of Chaucer and Spenser.

Miss Anna *Seward.* Anna *Seward* (12 December 1747–25 March 1809) was an English Romantic poet, often referred to as the Swan of Lichfield. Born at Eyam in Derbyshire, she spent nearly all her life in Lichfield, beginning at an early age to write poetry, partly at the instigation of Erasmus Darwin. Her verses include numerous elegies — so many that Sir Walter Scott was said to have been reluctant to edit her works while she yet lived, lest she end up composing one for *him.* After her death, Scott edited Seward's *Poetical Works* in three volumes (1810). To these he prefixed a memoir of the author, along with extracts from her literary correspondence. He declined, however, to include the bulk of her letters, and these were published in six volumes by A. Constable as *Letters of Anna Seward 1784–1807* (Edinburgh, 1811). Her connections with Dr Johnson are documented in a variety of sources, but see especially Margaret Ashmun's *The Singing Swan: An Account of Anna Seward and her Acquaintance with Dr Johnson, Boswell, and others of their Time* (1931).

'Invidia gloriae comes': Envy is a companion to glory.

Reverend Mr *Chapman,* Vice-Chancellor of OXFORD UNIVERSITY. Joseph *Chapman,* graduate of Trinity College (1763); DD, 1777, served as Proctor (1775), President (1776–1808), and Vice-Chancellor (1784–8).

THE EAGLE AND CHILD. The Eagle and Child is a public house in St Giles's, Oxford, which is owned by St John's College, Oxford. It had been part of an endowment belonging to University College since the seventeenth century. The first record of its name is from 1684, and is said to derive from the crest of the Earl of Derby. The image is alleged to refer to a story of a noble-born baby having been found in an eagle's nest. The pub's long-standing nickname is 'the Bird and Baby'.

'O tempora, o mores!': 'Oh, the times! Oh, the customs!' This sentence by Cicero in found in his First Oration against Catiline, which TOBY mentions having studied with Dr Adams.

'aut disce aut discede': one must either 'learn or leave'; this was the motto of the old Cathedral School at St Paul's, as well as of various later educational establishments.

'Docendo discimus, mi alme sus': 'By your pupils you are taught, my dear pig!' The first part of this is a well-known Latin saw.

Mr Maurice *Morgann.* Maurice *Morgann* (1725–1802) was a government administrator and literary scholar, in the latter field of which he was renowned for his ingenious 'Essay on the character of Falstaff'. He once had the opportunity of entertaining Johnson for a day or two at Wickham, when its lord was absent, of which two anecdotes are related by *Boswell*:

> The first is not a little to the credit of Johnson's candour. Mr Morgann and he had a dispute pretty late at night, in which Johnson would not give up, though he had the wrong side, and in short, both kept the field. Next morning, when they met in the breakfasting-room, Dr Johnson accosted Mr Morgann thus: 'Sir, I have been thinking on our dispute last night —. You were in the right.'
>
> The second was as follows: Johnson, for sport perhaps, or from the spirit of contradiction, eagerly maintained that Derrick had merit as a writer. Mr Morgann argued with him directly, in vain. At length he had recourse to this device: 'Pray, Sir, (said he,) whether you do reckon Derrick or Smart the best poet?' Johnson at once felt himself roused; and answered, 'Sir, there is no settling the point of precedency between a louse and a flea.'

TOBY apparently encountered Mr Morgann at the same place (Wickham) where these debates were said to have taken place.

'absque labore, nihil': nothing without labour.

Mr *Lockyer.* Has not been identified. There were numerous public houses and inns of this period also known as the 'White Hart'.

Sir Joseph *Banks.* Sir Joseph *Banks,* 1st Baronet, GCB, PRS (13 February 1743–19 June 1820), was an English naturalist, botanist and eminent patron of the natural sciences. The son of a successful doctor, he attended Oxford, where he excelled in natural science; in 1764 he came into his inheritance and used his own money to fund expeditions to Newfoundland and Labrador. On his return, he accompanied Captain James Cook on his first great voyage from 1768 to 1771. His energy and expense in obtaining biological specimens was unparalleled, and in 1778 he was elected President of the Royal Society, an office which he retained until his death thirty-two years later. Throughout this time, he lent his support to voyages of exploration to every corner of the world, and as a result his name has been given to places all about the globe, among them Banks Island in the Canadian Arctic, Cape Banks in Australia, and Banks Peninsula on the South Island of New Zealand.

Mr John *Sheldon's* ANATOMICAL MUSEUM. This was John Sheldon, Anatomist and Surgeon (1752–1808), whose museum was, at the time of this narrative, located in Tottenham Court Road, London. According to an 1899 account, 'Sheldon was desirous of devoting himself to scientific investigation and to teaching rather than to practice. He, however, became surgeon to the Medical Asylum in Welbeck Street, and in 1786 was appointed surgeon to the Westminster Hospital. Sheldon succeeded William Hunter as lecturer on Anatomy to the Royal Academy in 1782, and was the author of an important work on the lymphatics. His style was lucid, and his published writings stamp him as probably having been an excellent teacher.'

Dr William *Cullen.* Dr William *Cullen,* FRS, FRSE, FRCPE (1710–89), was perhaps the most distinguished among TOBY's circle of friends and supporters, and the only one to have contributed directly to his *Memoirs,* by the addition of his personal endorsement. Cullen was born in Hamilton, Lanarkshire, into a professional family; educated at the University of Glasgow, he served as an apothecary's apprentice and a ship's surgeon before arriving at the University of Edinburgh in 1734. After completing his studies, in addition to his usual medical duties, he pursued a strong interest in chemistry; in 1747 he was awarded a lectureship in chemistry, the first in Britain; in 1751 he ascended to a professorship in the Practice of Medicine. He was instrumental in obtaining a Royal Charter for the Philosophical Society of Edinburgh, and laid the cornerstone of the new College of Surgeons building. To his warm and generous character, there are innumerable testimonies; one mark of his humility and dedication to his work may also be seen in the fact that, although elected to the Royal Society in London, he never managed to find the time to visit and sign the official register. Indeed, his appearance and decisive ruling in the case of TOBY's trial were apparently the cause of his first and only visit to London.

Mr *Lingham,* THE ACADEMY ROOM, LYCEUM. According to *The Harmonicon* (1830),

This place of amusement, previously to its having become a fixed and permanent theatre, as it at length appears to be, has, perhaps, had as many tenants, and undergone as many transmutations, as any place of the kind in the kingdom. When the Society of Artists was incorporated in the year 1765, James Payne, Esq., an eminent architect, purchased this part of the ground belonging to Exeter House, on which he built an elegant fabric, as a Lyceum, or Academy and Exhibition-room, to anticipate the Royal establishments then in contemplation; and several exhibitions afterwards took place . . . in the 1780s, the premises, which were large, and certainly eligible for the purpose, were converted to their present use, under the auspices of their then landlord, the late Mr *Lingham,* a breeches-maker, of the Strand, by whom they had been recently purchased. Admission, 2*s.* 6*d.* and 1*s.*

Charles *Dibdin.* Charles *Dibdin* (*c.* 4 March 1745–25 July 1814) was a British musician, dramatist, actor and songwriter. The son of a parish clerk, he was intended by his parents for the Church, and so was sent to Winchester. However, his love of music diverted his thoughts from the clerical profession, and he went to London at the age of fifteen, where he became a singing actor at Covent Garden. In 1762 his first work, a pastoral operetta entitled *The Shepherd's Artifice,* for which he had written both words and music, was produced at this theatre. Other works followed, which firmly established his reputation, but despite his success, his love of the high life led him to fall deep into debt, to escape which he was obliged to flee to France for several years. In 1782 he became joint manager of the Royal Circus, which post he held when he served on TOBY's jury, but not long after, he lost this position owing to a quarrel with his partner. His later career consisted principally of one-man stage revues enacted at his own theatre, the *Sans Souci* in Leicester-place; he also obtained a modest income from writing his memoirs.

QUO USQUE TANDEM: 'How much longer?' The first three words of a famous phrase of Cicero's, from his First Oration; the full sentence reads, *'Quo usque tandem abutere, Catilina, patientia nostra'* — 'How much longer, Catiline, will you abuse our patience?'

'Sine omnia regula': literally, 'without any rules'. This is from Dante's *De Vulgari Eloquentia,* his defence of eloquence in the vernacular.

Mr William *Wilberforce.* William *Wilberforce* (24 August 1759–29 July 1833) was a British politician, philanthropist and leader of the movement to abolish the slave trade. A native of Hull, he began his political career in 1780, when he was elected Member of Parliament for Yorkshire. In 1787, he came into contact with a group of anti-slave-trade activists, among them Granville Sharp, Hannah More and Charles Middleton. From that point forth, Wilberforce took on the cause of abolition, heading the parliamentary campaign against the British slave trade for twenty-six years until the passage of the Slave Trade Act in 1807. He also championed causes as diverse as free schools for the poor, missionary work in India, and the creation of a colony in Sierra Leone. Late in his life, he was one of the founders of what became the Royal Society for the Prevention of Cruelty to Animals — which last, it is hard to resist concluding, must have had something to do with his early encounter with TOBY and his less fortunate namesake.

Mr John *Fawkes*/Mr *Schmidt.* Of the details of this man's life, we know little beyond what TOBY tells us, although it is remarkable to note that an old handbill of his survived to catch the attention of Charles Dickens many years later:

The earliest account that we have seen of a learned pig is to be found in an old Bartholomew Fair bill, issued by that Emperor of all conjurors, Mr Fawkes, which exhibits the portrait of the swinish pundit holding a paper in his mouth, with the letter Y inscribed upon it. This 'most amazing pig' which had a particularly early tail, was the pattern of docility and sagacity: the 'Pig of Knowledge, Being the only one ever taught in England'. He was to be visited 'at a Commodious Room, at the George, West-Smithfield, During the time of the Fair' and the spectators were required to 'See and Believe!' Three-pence was the price of admission to behold 'This astonishing animal' perform with cards, money and watches, &c. &c. The bill concluded with a poetical apotheosis to the pig, from which we extract one verse:

A learned pig in George's reign,
To Æsop's brutes an equal boast;
Then let mankind again combine,
To render friendship still a toast.

Stella said that Swift could write sub-limely upon a broomstick. Who ever, as the Methodists say, better 'improved' a pig, except by roasting it! Mr Fawkes had also earlier exhibited a 'learned goose' in a room opposite the George Inn, West-Smithfield. (Bentley's *Miscellany,* Vol. 9).

Mr *Hughes's* ROYAL CIRCUS; the Automaton Pig; Signor *Spinetti.* Ricky Jay, in his *Learned Pigs and Fireproof Women* (1986), recounts that 'a Mr Hughes, Proprietor of the Royal Circus, had as early as 1785 exhibited an automaton Pig of Knowledge as well as a mechanical monkey who did evolutions on a tight-rope; both were presented by Signor Spinetti'; this is confirmed in Thomas Frost's *Lives of the Conjurors* (1876).

Sieur *Garman* and his 'Cochon Savant'. This rival is also noted in Ricky Jay's *Learned Pigs and Fireproof Women* (1986) as appearing at Astley's London establishment.

Mr *Flaxman,* Mr William *Blake.* John *Flaxman* (6 July 1755–7 December 1826) was an English sculptor and draughtsman. Born in the city of York, he showed an interest in art from an early age; as a child, he was said to carry about with him a quantity of wax so that he could take an impression of every button or seal he encountered. He studied at the Royal Academy and secured a position making models for Wedgwood's china manufactory. He later travelled throughout Italy for a number of years, returning with a high reputation as a sculptor, which earned him numerous commissions. He became good friends with the young William Blake, and apparently persuaded his aunt and uncle, who operated a bookshop in the Strand just a few doors down from the Lyceum, to print the volume mentioned here — Blake's first book of poetry — *Poetical Sketches,* in 1783.

William *Blake* (28 November 1757–12 August 1827) was an English poet, painter and printmaker. Trained as an engraver, his artistic and poetic gifts were encouraged by a close circle of friends, among them Flaxman and the Reverend Henry Mathew. From 1787 onwards, Blake self-published small, exquisite editions of his poetry in the form of 'illuminated books' engraved on copperplate; although admired by those who knew them, they attracted but slight attention from critics or the public. Blake died in 1827 in poverty and obscurity, and his poems received critical acclaim only long after his death. Today his verse is widely regarded as among the most enduring of the Romantic era, and his paintings have led one contemporary art critic to proclaim him 'far and away the greatest artist Britain has ever produced'. Blake's references to the 'learned pig' and the 'hare playing on a tabor' in the following verse would seem to corroborate TOBY's intimations of familiarity:

Give Pensions to the Learned Pig,
Or the Hare playing on a Tabor;
Anglus can never see Perfection
But in the Journeyman's Labour.

Mr John *Tipping. The Court leet records of the manor of Manchester: from the year 1552 to the Year 1686, and from the Year 1731 to the Year 1846* lists Mr John Tipping as one of the Constables for Manchester as of 1762, and it is entirely possible that he later served again in this position.

'*Tempus fugit, non autem memoria*': 'Time flies, but not in memory.'

Mrs *Siddons.* Sarah *Siddons* (5 July 1755–8 June 1831) was a British actress, the best-known tragedienne of the eighteenth century. She was the elder sister of John Philip Kemble, Charles Kemble, Stephen Kemble, Ann Hatton and Elizabeth Whitlock, and the aunt of Fanny Kemble. She was most famous for her portrayal of the Shakespearean character Lady Macbeth. The Sarah Siddons Society continues to present the Sarah Siddons Award in Chicago every year to a prominent actress.

Mr *Frazer's* DANCING ESTABLISHMENT, Glasgow. See the description of TOBY's appearance at this establishment given above under Samuel *Nicholson.* Mr Frazer appears to have opened his Academy in 1781 (*Glasgow Mercury,* 11 October 1781). About its proprietor, alas, the present Editor has thrown up his own hands in *frustration,* there being so little information on him that he can make no other gesture.

'A Pair of Italians'. This story is given in *Cassell's Old and New Edinburgh* (1882), Vol. II, in terms so similar to those used by TOBY that it seems very likely that it drew upon TOBY's narrative for its source. Despite considerable exertions in that direction, the present Editor has been unable to ascertain the identity of these nameless Italians.

Jamie. Alas, TOBY does not give his friend's family name, and my exertions in the records of the University from this period have produced far too many candidates, the name or its variants (it was commonly used as a diminutive of 'James') being quite common.

Robert *Burns.* Robert *Burns* (25 January 1759–21 July 1796), also known as Rabbie Burns, the Ploughman Poet, and the Bard of Ayrshire, was a Scottish poet and lyricist. During his lifetime, much was made of his humble origins, and there can be little doubt of the shock felt in 1786 when the first volume of his verse appeared; as Chambers's *Cyclopedia* noted in 1851, 'Its influence was immediately felt, and is still operating on the whole imaginative literature of the kingdom.' The poet found his sudden rise to fame difficult, yet nearly all contemporary accounts testify, as does TOBY here, to his great personal humility and charm.

The Countess's Invitation. This anecdote is related by many biographers of Burns, among them John Lockhart (*Life of Robert*

Burns, 1830) and Alan Cunningham (*Life of Burns,* 1820). The name of the woman who issued the invitation is not given; she is sometimes identified as a 'Countess' and elsewhere simply as 'a certain stately Peeress'.

Sir James *Stirling,* Lord Provost of Edinburgh. *Cassell's Old and New Edinburgh* (Vol. IV, p. 282) describes him thus: 'Sir James *Stirling,* Bart., elected Lord Provost, afterwards Elder of Forneth, had a stormy time when in office. He was the son of a fishmonger at the head of Marlin's Wynd, where his sign was a wooden Black Bull, now in the Antiquarian Museum. Stirling, after being secretary to Sir Charles Dalling, Governor of Jamaica, became a partner in the bank of Mansfield, Ramsay, and Co. in Cantore's Close, Luckenbooths, and married the daughter of the head of the firm.' It may be noted here that, at this time, the Lord Provost of Edinburgh was also the nominal head of the University, it having not yet separated from municipal control.

Dr *Monro.* Alexander Monro *secundus* (22 May 1733–2 October 1817) was the son of the eminent anatomist Alexander Munro, known as *primus.* He was particularly well known for his *Observations on the Structure and Functions of the Nervous System* (1783).

John *Home*. John *Home* (22 September 1722–5 September 1808) was a Scottish poet and dramatist. He was born at Leith, near Edinburgh, where his father, Alexander Home, a distant relation of the earls of Home, was town clerk. John was educated at the Leith Grammar School, and at the University of Edinburgh, where he graduated MA in 1742. His first play, *Agis: a tragedy,* founded on Plutarch's narrative, was finished in 1747. He took it to London, and submitted it to David Garrick for representation at Drury Lane, but it was rejected as unsuitable for the stage. Never the less, a great number of his plays were produced in Edinburgh with success. Home died at Merchiston Bank, near Edinburgh, in his eighty-sixth year. He is buried in South Leith Parish Church. *The Works of John Home* were collected and published by Henry Mackenzie in 1822.

Curiously, the poem attributed to him by TOBY does not appear among Home's published verse, although there is a very similar (but not identical) stanza in Philip Frenau's 'Address to a Learned Pig', published in his collected works in 1809:

Science! — to You, that opens all her
    store?
Already have you in your sapient brain
More than most aldermen — and
    gumption more
Than some, who capers cut on Congress'
    floor.
May we not hope, in this improving age
Of human things — to see on Terra's
    stage!
Hogs take the lead of men, and from their
    styes
To honours, riches, office, rise!

It is the opinion of the present Editor that
TOBY's version is a far better one, and that
Mr Freneau — whose verse is sadly deficient
in numbers — must have had it in hand,
and used it as the source for his far more
'doggerel' version.

Mr Joseph *Black.* Joseph *Black,* FRSE FRCS
(16 April 1728–6 December 1799), was a
Scottish physician, known for his work with
James Watt on early steam-driven engines,
as well as his experiments with carbon
dioxide, which he called 'fixed air'. He
began his studies at Edinburgh in 1750, taking his medical degree in 1755. After a
period spent teaching in Glasgow, he returned to Edinburgh in 1766 to take up the

post of Professor of Chemistry, which he held until his death. He is buried in Greyfriars Kirkyard.

Mr *Walker.* John *Walker* (1731–31 December 1803) was Professor of Natural History at the University of Edinburgh from 1779 to 1803. He was born in Edinburgh, his father the rector of the Canongate School, at which John received an excellent education; he attended the University of Edinburgh from 1746 to 1749 and took a degree in Divinity. Over the next decade, with the encouragement of Dr Cullen, he pursued a variety of chemical experiments, as well as studying natural history, including fieldwork in remote areas of the Highlands and Hebrides. After his appointment at the University, he set about reforming and updating the previous course of study, expanding the course of lectures to an entire year. The high estimate TOBY gives of Professor *Walker,* along with his willingness to alter or even set aside the system of *Linnaeus,* is corroborated by numerous other accounts.

Mr William *Greenfield.* William Greenfield (2 February 1755–28 April 1827) was, as TOBY states, Hugh Blair's assistant and successor as Professor of Rhetoric and *Belles*

Lettres. He enjoyed quite a brilliant career until he was abruptly dismissed for 'an offence unnamed though known to be immoral conduct'. The unfortunate Greenfield was excommunicated from the Church of Scotland and retired into obscurity, with Blair resuming his former seat.

Dugald *Stewart.* Dugald *Stewart* (22 November 1753–11 June 1828), an influential Scottish philosopher, was born in Edinburgh. He was the son of Matthew Stewart, Professor of Mathematics at the University of Edinburgh; when the elder Stewart became ill in 1772, he asked Dugald, then only nineteen, to serve as his substitute. Three years later, following his father's death, he was elected to replace him. In 1792 he published the first volume of the *Elements of the Philosophy of the Human Mind;* the second volume appeared in 1814, the third in 1827. The opinions as to the state and educability of animals that TOBY ascribes to him are accurate quotations from Stewart's *Elements,* where they appear in section 106.

'Musco lapis volutus haud obvolvitur': attributed, as TOBY notes, to Publilius Syrus, this is more familiar in its English version: 'Moss grows not on a rolling stone.'

The False Autobiography. This was *The Life and Adventures of Toby the SAPIENT PIG, with his Opinions on Men and Manners. Embellished with an elegant frontispiece, descriptive of a literary pig sty, with the author in deep study* (London: *c.* 1805).

As we know he had a standing order with his bookseller, it is tempting to imagine that TOBY must have got hold of this book when it was new. This would date his death to some time after 1806 (but see note below). Some authorities, however, assign this volume to a later date, 1817, in connection with the flurry of appearances by its purported author, Mr Nicholas Hoare, in that year. It is possible that Hoare simply plagiarised an earlier volume; the language on his handbills (many of which advertise the book as well) is quite similar. This 'pamphlet' — at twenty-four pages, TOBY is correct in so calling it — was apparently written with tongue firmly in cheek, but our hero was unable to overcome the irritation that any other narrative, serious or facetious, might take the place of his own. A copy survives in the John Johnson collection of printed ephemera at the Bodleian Library, Oxford.

Laurie and Whittle's *New and Improved English Atlas, Divided into Counties*. This book, which appears to have been first issued in 1807, was one of the more compendious guides of its day, and was provided with numerous fold-out maps drawn by the eminent cartographer Benjamin Hoare. As the only specific book, other than the specious autobiography, that TOBY mentions by name, it has a certain pride of place. Its date, set alongside that of the porcine pamphlet, strongly suggests that TOBY could not have died *before* 1807 or thereabouts. His quotation from Goethe's *Faust*, which was first published in 1808, also points to his having survived at least to this period.

The ending of our narrative. Of the later years of our Hero, the historical record contains very little. Apparently, he continued to live in the rooms given him by Dr Cullen in Edinburgh; as noted above, there seems good circumstantial evidence for his having lived at least until 1809, which would put his age at twenty-eight. In the wild, pigs are said to have a life-span of roughly twenty-five years, and if that of the domestic pig is much shorter, it is usually because of causes of death other than those attributable to nature.

TOBY's *Memoir* was first published in

1809, and by his own account, it was very warmly received. Of the numerous later editions, many of them rife with all manner of spurious additions and emendations, the less said the better, although their number certainly attests to the book's widespread popularity. But perhaps the most fitting epitaph is that penned by Thomas Hood, and published in his *Comic Annual* for 1830. Although it was almost certainly inspired by a different learned pig (and there were by that time many latterday imitators), it never the less captures something of the feeling of TOBY's passing, and serves (I think) as a fitting conclusion to this volume. I give it here in its entirety:

THE LAMENT OF TOBY, THE LEARNED PIG

O heavy day! o day of woe!
To misery a poster,
Why was I ever farrow'd — why
Not spitted for a roaster?

In this world, pigs, as well as men.
Must dance to Fortune's fiddlings,
But must I give the classics up
For barley-meal and middlings?

Of what avail that I could spell
And read, just like my betters,
If I must come to this at last.
To litters, not to letters?

O, why are pigs made scholars of?
It baffles my discerning,
What griskins, fry, and chitterlings
Can have to do with learning.

Alas! My learning once drew cash.
But public fame's unstable,
So I must turn a pig again,
And fatten for the table.

To leave my literary line
My eyes get red and leaky;
But Giblett doesn't want me *blue,*
But red and white, and streaky.

Old Mullins used to cultivate
My learning like a gard'ner;
But Giblett only thinks of lard,
And not of doctor Lardner!

He does not care about my brain
The value of two coppers.
All that he thinks about my head
Is how I'm off for choppers.

Of all my literary kin
A farewell must be taken;
Good-bye to the poetic Hogg!
The philosophic Bacon!

Day after day my lessons fade,
My intellect gets muddy;
A trough I have, and not a desk,
A sty — and not a study!

Another little month, and then
My progress ends, like Bunyan's;
The seven sages that I loved
Will be chopp'd up with onions!

Then over head and ears in brine
They'll souse me, like a salmon;
My mathematics turned to brawn,
My logic into gammon.

My Hebrew will all retrograde,
Now I'm put up to fatten;
My Greek, it will go all to grease,
The Dogs will have my Latin.

Farewell to Oxford! and to Bliss!
To Milman, Crowe, and Glossop,
I now must be content with chats
Instead of learned gossip!

Farewell to 'Town'! farewell to 'Gown'!
I've quite outgrown the latter; —
Instead of trencher-cap, my head
Will soon be on a platter!

O, why did I at Brazen-Nose
Rout up the roots of knowledge?
A butcher that can't read will kill
A pig that's been to college!

For sorrow I could stick myself —
But conscience is a dasher;
A thing that would be rash in man
In me would be a rasher!

One thing I ask — when I am dead
And past the Stygian ditches —
And that is, Let my schoolmaster
Have one of my two Hitches.

'Twas he who taught my letters so
I ne'er mistook or miss'd 'em;
Simply by *ringing* at the nose,
According to *Bell's* system.

ACKNOWLEDGEMENT

The Editor would like to extend his thanks to those who were among TOBY's first and most devoted *Friends:* Mary Cappello and Jean Walton (in whose home this book first was read aloud), Brendan, Noah and Caeli Carr-Potter, Huw Lewis-Jones and Kari Herbert, Joe Zornado and Denise Leathers. For her persistent faith and skill in representing this book, I am indebted to my wonderful agent, Malaga Baldi. And to Jamie Byng, who at once understood and embraced TOBY's story, and has since worked with such extraordinary energy to bring it to the world at large, I will always be deeply grateful.

I would also like to thank my editor Jenny Lord, along with Norah Perkins, Hazel Orme and all the rest of the talented staff at Canongate Books. That TOBY's narrative is being published by a Press whose offices are — quite literally — a stone's throw from his actual home, seems to me almost an act of *Fate,* whose unpredictable fingers, sooner or later, manage to fit every Tale into its Telling. Thanks also to my classicist colleague Gary Grund for assistance with the *Latin* passages. And last, but very far from least, this book is for the *closest* of my Animal companions, Harvey and Chester.

ABOUT THE AUTHOR

Russell Potter teaches literature, early media, and the history of Arctic exploration. His most recent book is *Arctic Spectacles: The Frozen North in Visual Culture* and he was a presenter on the Emmy-nominated episode of PBS's *Nova,* "Arctic Passage: Prisoners of Ice." He lives in Providence, Rhode Island.